Jon Ferguson

The Flood

Huge Jam, 2022

In memory of my dear friend, Alain Imesch,
a Swiss doctor who surely would have survived
"the flood"...

1

Philip Papp walked to the window, whereupon he watched his hands unbuckle his belt. Then they unbuttoned and unzipped his pants and, with the ease of a nun's fingers removing her shoes in earlier days, dropped them and the drawers into a heap atop his thickly constituted ankles. He waited for a crowd to gather and maybe applaud. His apartment was on the first floor and it was a little past noon.

First a middle-aged woman and her son, eight going on eighty-eight, stopped on the sidewalk to admire his droopy fur-fraught dong.

"Look," the woman said, "one day you'll have a jewel like that."

"Oh," responded the boy. "Will it be so big?"

"It's not that big, dear. That's the way a lot of them get."

A few moments later an aged lady with a grey poodle leashed at her feet stopped next to them and smilingly craned her neck to get a view of Philip Papp. "I think I've seen this one before," she said. "Cute as a pickle." She rubbed the back of her neck with her free hand. The dog barked a bar of ugly high notes.

"Do you know him?" the younger woman asked.

"I think so. I don't usually forget my clients."

"What's your line of work?"

"Whoring."

"Really? That's cool."

"When my husband Raymond died I took it up. My granddaddy used to say that all women were either whores or housewives."

"Did he say that?"

"He also said that all men were either eels or eunuchs, and if they were eels, they were trying to slither their way into every crack in the ocean."

"When did your husband die?"

"Two years ago. Two weeks before my seventy-eighth birthday. We were going to celebrate it in New York City. He died, I buried him, and then I went to New York anyway. I decided that's what he would have wanted. I kept our same reservations, only it was now for one instead of two. I went to the museums, to Central Park and the Statue of Liberty, even up the Empire State

Building. Our...my...hotel wasn't far from Times Square and one afternoon I got to talking to the cutest girls on the sidewalk and the next thing you know I was in business. It helped me live without Raymond. So many women get cut in half when their husbands die and end up dying right after them. But I decided that wasn't for me."

"Well, good for you."

"Nice boy you've got there."

"That's my son Chipper. He wants to be a truck driver. Since he could talk those eighteen wheelers are all he wants to converse about."

"He might change his mind."

"I hope he doesn't. I always wanted a truck driver as a son."

Philip Papp turned from his frontal position to give passers-by a side view. He scratched his rear end gorilla-like then fingered his crotch. The younger woman noticed the yin-yang symmetry of the bulging belly and the oval butt.

"Look Mommy, that's the potato chip man!" A potato chip truck bounced down the street.

"That it is," his mother said.

"Let's go, Mommy. You promised we would go buy a watermelon."

"I did. But I'm talking to this nice woman here."

"Okay."

"Wonderful child."

"Yes, he is. So do you enjoy the whole whoring thing?"

"Quite. I try to keep it down to three eels a day. That's plenty for me."

"Three meals...three eels. That's a good one." The younger woman chuckled.

"It keeps me active and not wishing I were dead."

"Well, you look wonderful."

"I'm eighty. I never thought I'd live past seventy-eight. That's when my mother, and her mother before her, died."

"Well, I'm sure if they weren't dead they'd both be proud of you. If I look like you when I'm eighty, I'll know that at least I did something right in my life."

"Like what?"

"Kept the flies off me."

"Mommy, let's go."

"Okay, dear. It was nice talking to you. What was your name again?"

"I never said it, I don't think. Betty Swain. Raymond used to call me 'Swan'. Raymond loved my neck. And yours?"

"My neck?"

"No, your name."

"I'm Tamilia Lattner, but everybody calls me Tammy."

"Okay Tammy. It was nice talking to you."

"Do you live around here?"

"Not far. A few blocks away."

Another truck went by and little Chipper grabbed his mother's hand and pointed.

"Say goodbye to Mrs. Swain then."

"Goodbye Mrs. Swain."

They waltzed down the street hand in hand. The poodle barked at its end of the leash.

Philip Papp eyed all four of them. He wasn't getting the crowd he had expected.

Betty Swain thought she might go in and talk to him. Before she decided on doing anything, a foot patrolman in a swanky blue uniform strolled towards her and tipped his hat. "How's business, Betty? Ya keepin outta trouble?"

"Bill, I've never been in trouble. Eighty years on earth and the worst thing I've ever done was to forget to turn off the oven."

"Do you know Philip Papp?" the officer asked, glancing from the window to the blue sky.

"I'm not quite sure. I was just thinking that I might go knock on his door."

"Nice chap. His wife passed a couple years ago. He works for the city planners."

"Now I remember him. Three kids, right?"

"I think so.

"All grown up?"

"Yes."

"Yes, yes. Now I remember. His wife got hit by an ice-cream truck. The driver had a heart attack and took out some people at a crosswalk. Sure I know him. Yes, a real nice fellow. He was real sad when we first started talking. Didn't really want to talk at all. But I loosened him up with a couple of jokes and a cup of whiskey. We had a wonderful time. It must have been a year ago."

"That's Philip, all right."

"Maybe I'll just scoot up there and rustle up a little business. It's been a slow day. Saw Max Grundy this morning, but that's been all."

"How is Max?"

"He can't seem to find his cat is what he told me. I was trying to keep him from squirtin' his juice too quickly and all he wanted to talk about was his cat."

"Does he still have his wife?"

"Yes, yes. She was in the other room watching TV. Bitchy woman from what I've seen. Shouting at him to shut the door and keep it down."

"Poor guy must have had a short menu when he chose a wife."

"Probably didn't have a menu."

"Probably didn't."

"So how's the neighbourhood Bill? Everything spick-and-span?"

"Thanks to you, Betty."

"Bill, you could charm a tick off a dog's ass."

"Hell no. I just tell it like it is. We haven't had a problem in a month, not since the Fowler's dog killed that neighbour's cat. You know, Betty, I don't even know why we have police anymore. All I do is walk around and have fun talking to people like you."

"Just thank the flood, Bill. Just thank the flood."

"So it seems."

"So Bill, what do you think? Should I go up there and give Philip Papp a helping hand?"

Before answering, the policeman looked back up at the window where Philip had resumed the frontal position. "I wouldn't know what he needs. I used to think I knew what people needed, but I've come to the conclusion that most people themselves don't know what they need, so how the hell am I supposed to know?"

"You're right about that, Bill. What I do is I just flit around like a little bumblebee, from flower to flower, trying to bring a little honey into the world."

"You're no bumblebee. You're an angel, Betty."

"Still don't have any wings though. Just these old legs that are starting to tell me that the race is almost over."

"You got plenty of miles left."

"Don't count on it."

"Betty, I've never asked you how much you charge."

"I don't really charge. I leave it up to the customer. I never let him pay in advance. When I've finished my work, I let him pay me for what I was worth. Works for both of us."

"You got any free time today?"

"If I don't go up those stairs and see Philip Papp, free time is *all* I have today."

"Well, it's my lunch break in ten minutes."

"Mine too then, Bill."

2

The flood was a formality. It was the easiest way to get a load off my back. I got rid of two types, the believers and the coveters. I was sick and tired of them both. Especially the believers. I just couldn't take them anymore. Living lives of lies. They were of many sorts, but they all had two things in common: gods and afterlives. Can you imagine spending – wasting – the short time you have on the merry-go-round believing in things that are totally bogus? These poor people couldn't see and feel the earth at their feet because they were always looking up, up, up at a heaven that isn't there. Hundreds of gods, hundreds of different versions of the afterlife...O what a waste. What a sorry way to have spent the blink of an eye that was their time on earth.

And it wasn't only their gods, but also all those lists they made of thou shalts and thou shalt nots. I couldn't take them anymore either. They all had to go. The people and their damn lists. I sent the coveters with them for good measure, because they were a pain in *everybody's* ass.

Actually I probably should have wiped out both types a long time ago. But as my options are limited, I let them putter around for a few lousy millennia. You see, I am not God. I don't have that power and I don't have that clout. There is no God. As far as I can tell there never has been and there never will be. If I were a god, I can pretty much guarantee you that the last thing I would want is for my creations to worship me and pray to me. Now seriously, what kind of a god would want that? What kind of a god would put people on this crazy earth and then want them to spend their time prostrated like worms on a wet sidewalk worshipping and praying and sitting in some cold or stuffy church all day? No god would be so self-centred. No god would want that. How people came up with that kind of god in the first place is beyond me. (Well, not really beyond me. I've watched it for a few thousand years. Weak crops of humanity.) A real god would want people to be running around appreciating the beauty of life and sucking the last possible drop of juice out of this wild fruity earth before they died.

But all of this is neither here nor there, because there is no god and all the god worshippers are now gone. For the moment anyway. What there is, is me. Me and you, you that I spared. And my powers are simple. I've got two: I can give life and I can take it away. I can do nothing in between. I am like a farmer: I can plant the crops and I can destroy them. But what they grow into I cannot control. Wheat will be wheat, apples will be apples, corn will be corn, sunflowers will be sunflowers. Call me the Jolly Green Giant if you'd like because I'm really nothing more. I can only plant and harvest. I'm sorry if you expected more. But there is no more. Those who expected more are gone. And you are you. I gave you arms, legs, a head with what you call a brain or a spirit, a heart and blood, the heart to squirt the blood around and the blood to keep things alive, things like the kidneys and the livers, the lungs and the genitals and digestive tracts. You are what you are and are nothing more. You enjoy being you and I enjoy being me. Neither of us will be anything other.

You know, it is a curious thing that before the flood people never guessed correctly as to my nature and identity. Some got close, but they always ended up attributing qualities and powers to me that I didn't have. They wanted me omniscient, the great Know-It-All. Interesting idea, but a human, so human, invention. The concept "knowing" is itself a human invention. Pure knowledge is like pure soup or pure spaghetti bolognese or pure rainwater. It is never pure. It is always tainted by what it is. We all – me included – feel our way through life doing what we can with what we have. Dogs do it. Spiders do it. Trees do it. Worms do it. Kings did it. Ants do it. Doctors do it. Monkeys do it. Slaves did it. Lions do it. Butterflies do it. What we do is not based on pure knowledge. It is based on survival and trying to get what we want. We have no real perspective. We think we do, but we don't. We all live in the tiny world of our own time and our own place. I last longer than you, that's all. But I, too, am what I am and nothing more. And omni-science is not part of what I am.

But back to those people before the flood and their desire for a god or gods to lay down pages and pages of moral imperatives. Thou shalt do this and thou shalt not do that because if you do or don't do your destiny will be heaven or hell. These poor blind people believing that good and evil were written into the fabric of life, so blind that they didn't realise that what was good for one was evil for another and vice versa. "Thou shalt not eat pigs" one man shouted from the top of a hill, saying that the words came from the mouth of God. "Thou shalt not eat cows," bellowed another from another hilltop, also saying the words came through him from the tongue of God. "Thou shalt not eat meat of any kind," chimed another, he too saying his words were not his, but God's. And on and on and on this went. All over the world. All over the world people made laws that fitted their situations and they all said they came from God. Poor, bewildered, abused God. But they didn't come from God. They came from people. There are no moral laws written into the fabric of life. The history of humanity prior to the flood was the history of moralities that suited the humans that made them. "Thou shalt do this" because doing this gets me, the lawmaker, what I want and gets me where I want to go. "Thou shalt not kill" means that thou shalt not kill what I don't want you to kill. But what I want you to kill thou shalt kill or thine ass is in trouble. "Thou shalt have as many wives as thou want," one lawmaker says. "Thou shalt have no more than five wives," another declares. "No, thou shalt have only one wife," a third proclaims with a voice loud and clear. But if thou want to be really clean and really pure, "Thou shalt have no wife at all!" cries another commander of law.

And on and on went the moral merry-go-round until I decided on the flood. The survivors knew that morality was their own code and not God's.

Let's be clear about something else here. I, the Jolly Green Giant, am deserving of absolutely no praise or adoration. I didn't do anything to be who I am. I just am, like the rest of the universe. I'm just here. I did not make myself any more than the sun made itself or the moon made itself or the ice cream vendor made himself. I happen to be the farmer. You happen to be my crops. Other farmers have their crops. I plant people. They plant tomatoes. The tomatoes get ripe or rotten, they pick them or throw them away. The people piss me off too much, I send a flood. So that's what I did. But don't curse me and don't praise me. Just be glad I let you stick around. Millions have come and millions have gone. Consider yourself fortunate. Breathe while you can.

Hold on a second. I can see some of you bouncing in your chairs thinking that if I can create people, then somebody can create me. Believe me, I've looked around. I looked for a "few billion years", to use your pitiful time scheme. I even did the worship and pray thing for a while, just hoping something would show up. But nothing came. Zilch. Nada. Niente. Nothing showed up. Nothing manifested even the slightest interest. Nothing else was in the woodwork, or under the rug, or hiding in the cracks outside of time and space. So, I finally came to the rather lonely conclusion that this was it; what is is; what isn't isn't; what is can be nothing other than what it is. Stars explode, moons turn, tornadoes tear up towns and fields, children play, people go to work, dogs bark, cats meow, cows chew grass, people kill cows, the sun shines, the rain falls, people yearn, birds eat worms and build nests, people build buildings, clouds form, clouds break apart, the farmers plants their seeds.

Now don't fidget. I can see you fidgeting and saying,

"But why, why did you wait so long? Why haven't you told the world before? Why didn't you tell the people before the flood? Why your silence up until now?" Two reasons. A: before the flood nobody would have believed me, and B: I couldn't find a publisher. Before the flood I sent manuscripts to dozens of publishing houses. They all gave me the dead weenie. Many of them didn't even have the courtesy to answer. Most of them sent a single paragraph photocopied answer. But it didn't really matter because back then people would have thought I was a crackpot.

In any case, what the hell difference does it make if it was then or now? What was was, what is is, and what will be will be. I do my thing and you do yours.

3

Betty Swain took Bill the policeman back to her place and started out by showing him her orchids. "Touch them, Bill," she said. "Touch them." Bill touched them and then she touched Bill.

When Bill left, Betty thought for a moment and didn't know what to do. She counted the money Bill had put on the table. Thirty dollars. She made herself some tea. It was only two o'clock, but she was thirsty, somewhat tired, and unsure if she would take a nap or go back outside. She sipped the tea where she always sipped her tea, to wit, at the dining room table facing a picture of herself and Raymond in their wedding get up. The picture had no nostalgic effect on Betty Swain. She simply liked to see Raymond's smile, his wavy hair, and the look in her eyes. It was the look of love.

Betty had grown up in a family that called themselves Christians. But she realised quite young that they were not. They thought America was God's chosen country; Betty knew neither Christ nor his father would ever choose one country over another. They also tended not to like people who didn't act like they did: Jesus liked everybody. They talked a lot about making money: Jesus never talked about making money nor did he ever try to get rich. So, Betty divined, they weren't Christ-like Christians. Betty was fifteen when she decided that there was no point in being a Christian if you weren't Christ-like. She tried a little Buddha, Lao Tzu and Confucius, but she finally decided, after college, at age twenty-two, to just be Betty and to believe in nothing other than what was before her eyes and hands. She met Raymond that same year. He thought a lot like she did. They had a great time eating, drinking, talking, being merry, and making love. They got married and had one child. The child died in a boating accident at age sixteen. Actually the child was behind the boat, water-skiing. He fell and got tangled up in the rope. Before the driver of the boat knew what had happened, he had been pulled under the water and dragged a couple of hundred yards. When the boat finally stopped and the child got picked up, he was a limp, water-logged mass. Betty and Raymond mourned with thick spouting tears. But they decided to keep on living.

Years later, they both survived the flood. Of course, their son's death had had nothing to do with the flood. It had been a consequence of inattention.

Betty survived Raymond.

She sipped her tea to the hum of the refrigerator. She took a nap.

Bill was back on the beat. He felt refreshed and when he glanced at the sky he saw, looking to the east, in the fleece of a massive cumulus, a face that reminded him of a sheep.

4

How many people died in the flood? A lot. Close to eighty-five percent. But there were getting to be too many of you anyway. At least in some places. Don't forget, the coveters went as well. You're asking what I mean by coveters? Simple answer. The people who wanted other people's stuff. Anything: money, shoes, jewellery, house, wife, husband, friend, car, bicycle, meal, seat at the ball game. Whatever. You name it, somebody usually wanted it. Of course common thieves drowned. But other coveters went, too. Lots of people who had never taken anything from anybody – often because their religion forbade it – were snuffed as well. People who spent their time wishing they had other people's things or situations went too. I figured that they were never going to enjoy being who they were so I threw them in for good measure. Interestingly, a lot of people who had very little were among the survivors. But most of these people had little technology: make of that what you will. The people who had a lot got washed away at a much higher rate.

So I thought we'd try a new world. No more believers in afterlives and gods and no more people who weren't happy with who they were and what they had. A rather simple equation. I don't know why I hadn't thought of it before.

Naturally some cultures and countries lost huge chunks of their populations. You can imagine which ones they were. But every region had its survivors and every region seems to be doing quite well for the moment. Enough buildings and houses were left so the survivors didn't have to start from scratch. Basically, they just had to clean up the mess. Sometimes they had to move to new quarters and start up what they were doing before in a different location.

It was interesting to watch the survivors figure out why those who had survived survived. But little by little they realised that none of them was taking up position behind a pulpit or pew and there were no thieves or general pains in the ass among them.

Naturally all the survivors were allowed to keep their children up to age sixteen. And naturally again, some of them are probably going to grow up to be coveters or believers in afterlives. But we're not there yet. The flood was only three years ago.

5

When Philip Papp waddled away from the window, his pants and drawers were still around his ankles. The couch was only a few feet away and, for whatever reason, he displaced himself in a duck-like fashion and fell onto the couch with a thud. He started fondling his warm soft pecker. He knew he needed some relief but didn't know if he could bring it upon himself. As it turned out, this time he wasn't able to, so he went to the phone and called Betty Swain. He had watched her walk away with Bill the policeman, but he didn't know she was taking him home. The phone rang, but Betty had graciously turned it off on her end.

Philip Papp's wife had not gone in the flood, but a few months after. She contracted some kind of rare cancer that sent her rather quickly to the cemetery. Philip was crushed and still is. He is the kind of guy who knows when he has a good thing and his wife, Angela, had been a good thing. She had massaged his back and feet after work, had raised their three children – two girls and a boy – with a smile on her face, had cooked meals that tasted like they came out of a garden, had kept a house that was a pleasant balance between tidy and relaxed, and had given him regular sexual pleasure throughout the greater part of their thirty years together. He couldn't find a way or a person to replace her. Exposing himself at the window sometimes took a little out of the pressure cooker, but it had become less and less effective. Beating his meat, however tenderly or aggressively, had never been a satisfactory answer. He didn't love Betty Swain, or for that matter any of the other younger whores in the neighbourhood all of whom were very pleasant to be around. The truth was, they didn't love him either, so that equation was naturally never going to produce a lasting solution. But for the moment he was only seeking temporary relief.

Philip Papp's grown children all survived the flood thanks to their education. They had been raised in an atmosphere of tolerance for their religiously inclined friends and neighbours, their parents teaching them that nobody asked to be born into the family they were born into and that to look down on a kid because it believed its parents was no help to anybody. They themselves had never set foot in a church. The Papp family had celebrated Christmas until Angela died, but only did it for the tree, the lights, the beautiful carols, the delicate exchange of gifts, and the turkey dinner. The children all lived hundreds or thousands of miles away and Philip, though he loved them, was not the kind of person to pressure them to come back to help him fight his loneliness. He was a gentle man with a limp prick in his hand that, since Angela's death, he had often wished had been cut off or would simply disappear.

He fell asleep on the sofa. On waking at three that afternoon he called Betty Swain again. She said she'd be by in a jiffy.

6

When I think back on the state of things before the flood I want to laugh and cry at the same time. The waste, the waste of time, life, and energy of so many millions of human beings believing in gods that were no more real than the heroes in comic books; the guilt, the feelings of self-disgust that so ate at the hearts of so many because they saw themselves as other than perfect; the fact that this world was so overlooked because so many eyes were set on an afterlife, another higher, better world that...that simply isn't there; the killing in the name of that higher and better world; the fact that people – supposed "thinkers" – saw themselves to be outside of nature, to be outside of "the natural" world. (Before the flood, if you asked someone what nature was, they'd point to flowers and birds and trees and birds' nests, but never at themselves and the cities and things they'd built. Why?

Because all that was seen as outside of nature. This was humankind's major error. This opened the door for the belief that there was another world waiting. The failure to see that a person's place in the world was no different than the spider's or grasshopper's or eagle's. The hate and disgust of people who thought other people were "below" them because they neither believed in their gods nor followed the "thou shalts" and the "thou shalt nots" of the preachers of these gods of bad air who, though invisible, were built higher and higher and inflated bigger and bigger and finally took up so much space that there was no space left for this world. The lack of vision: not the vision of looking to the moons and stars and galaxies that float infinitely in the finite, but the lack of vision when looking at each other, the lack of depth in seeing that a woman or a man, that all women and men, remained innocent as the babies freshly pushed from their mothers' wombs they'd all once been. People come into the world and go to the grave never asking to have the body and mind that they have, never knowing why their mind "chooses" what it chooses – what it doesn't choose – because it in fact doesn't choose, choice being a word invented for humans but not for the rest of nature. The judgement, watching people punish each other for acts that were no different than a tree falling on someone in a forest or a cow fornicating in a pasture...we don't punish a tree or a cow, we deal with it, we avoid it when we can and we put it out of its misery when it is too miserable to live... But we don't punish it. Terms such as punishment and justice and injustice are simply leftovers from a more barbaric age, an age that invented the terms. When you look at the world under a microscope do you see freedom? When you look at the brain or the heart under a microscope, is it freedom you see? Freedom is a word that people invented to feel superior to the rest of nature. All of that is the legacy children inherit. So that is why I want to both laugh and especially cry when I look back on the ante-diluvian world.

I can see and hear you sitting in your chairs and asking, "But if people are not responsible for who they are, why did you get rid of eighty-five percent of them? Why did you kill so many?" A good question. But I have a good answer. I was tired of them. I didn't punish them as the Bible narrates; I just took them away. I wanted a different world. I can plant and I can harvest. I harvested. Most die without my intervention. I have the first word, and sometimes, when I feel the need, I have the last word too.

7

"Good afternoon Philip."

"Hi Betty. Thanks for coming."

"It's my pleasure. I saw you standing at the window around noontime. I almost came up then."

"I saw you walk away with Bill. I thought you were going home, but when I called there was no answer."

"I did go home. But Bill came with me so I turned the phone off for the duration."

"I like Bill a lot. He's a friend."

"He likes you."

"Who was that woman and child you were with? She was cute."

"Her name was Tammy something. Child's name was Chipper. Said he wanted to be a truck driver. They were real pleasant. First time I've met them."

"Betty...Betty, standing at the window doesn't help like it used to. I guess I was always hoping that Angela would see me and maybe she would just come right through the door or the window, but of course she never did."

"Angela died how many years ago?"

"Almost three. Just after the flood."

"If there's one thing I've learned in my eighty years on this earth it's that what we really love will never, ever leave us. We carry it around like an arm or a leg. Angela must have been a lovely woman."

"She was."

"How are your children doing? I can't remember where you said they are."

"I have a daughter in Portland who followed her husband out there when he got a job with a big shoe company. She works as a secretary. My other daughter is in Arizona. She's got a couple of young kids and her husband is a firefighter. My son is down in Florida. In fact, he called this morning saying he had a new girlfriend. He's my youngest...twenty-five. He said something about his girlfriend being sixteen. He works for a company that makes airplane seats."

"Sounds like everybody is doing well."

"They seem to be. Nobody is hungry."

"Would you like a cup of whiskey? I have some fine stuff from Ireland."

"That would be nice."

Betty Swain opened her oversized handbag and removed a bottle. She went to the kitchen and came back with two cups. Philip's she filled half full. She poured an inch for herself. "Here you are," she said. Philip took the cup and spread himself out on the green sofa. He held it with two hands like a young child would and sipped it slowly, his hands slightly trembling. Betty sat down next to his hip and began massaging his bulged belly with her free hand. When she finished her cup, only ten minutes were needed to take some of the pressure out of the loins that Philip Papp shared, unpleasantly these days, with himself.

8

There was another thing I was tired of seeing. So many of the planet's people had become spectators. Instead of living their own lives, they would spend half their time watching others. They had to be entertained because they were incapable of doing things themselves. When I put people on the earth, I like to see them act. I like to see them create, invent, smell flowers, walk in the mountains, farm, pick tomatoes, swim in the gorgeous savage sea. But before the flood so many people had become stuck to chairs watching screens or walking around, while seated, in a meta-verse. They spent hours every day like that. Their pleasures were vicarious and vicarious pleasures are always watered down. I didn't need to make up a third category to go with the believers and coveters; most of the watchers fitted into one of the two, or both.

Another group that I had seen way too much of were athletes that prayed to God or crossed themselves before entering the playing field somehow thinking that God would protect or favour them over their opponents in some meaningless sporting event. Fortunately for him or her, God was not there to be the brunt of such a base humiliation. In soccer in Europe, the number of times I saw a player score a goal then prance around pointing a finger skyward as if to say that God was with him was enough to make me want to vomit. And in those post-game interviews in America where coaches and athletes declared with straight faces that they "just thank God" for the chance to be where they are, that is, in the semi-finals or finals of some meaningless tournament watched by fiftymillionpeopleeatingpotatochipsandgulpingbeeronco uches.

The flood brought some fresh air to a pale stale world.

9

When Bill went back on the beat after blithely bartering with Betty, he had a graceful grin on his face. He exuded satisfaction for close to an hour. Betty had told him to close his eyes and dream of whatever he wanted to dream about while she put her slightly arthritic fingers to work to loosen him up, tickle the pinkish side of his soul, and eventually count all the way down to a limp lift-off. Bill knew where Betty was taking him. He followed her lead like a prancing dog and when Betty said "Five... Four...Three...Two...One..." Bill was right in step.

But after an hour he felt himself sliding back into his standard state wherein he sensed he was missing something. Bill the policeman tried to love all the world all the time, but some little pulling or pushing in his gut always brought him back to wanting something that he didn't have.

When Bill was thirty-three – ten years before the flood – he had a vision one day while pushing his shopping cart out of the grocery store towards his angled parked car. He stopped in mid-stroll and thought suddenly that it was very likely that essentially everything he had ever been taught about life and the world was probably a lie. He thought first of how, when he was young, people were saying that the earth was 7,000 years old. A few years later in junior high his teachers said it was 50,000 years old. In high school, three years later, his science teacher said it was 1,000,000 years old. When he got to college the world's first birthday party was thought to be 4,000,000 years prior. That morning in the newspaper he had read an article saying it all started about 5,000,000,000 years ago. In thirty years people supposedly in the know had gone from thousands to millions to billions. What shocked him was that they all talked like they knew what they were talking about. Obviously they didn't. In another hundred years, he thought, holding his ideas in his head and his shopping cart in his hands, they'll be saying mother earth is 6,000,000,000,000,000,000 years old. Why, he wondered right then and there in the parking lot, hadn't anybody suggested that maybe there was no beginning, and that all these efforts to give an age to the world were just sorry attempts to make life understandable for us idiots on earth. We seem to need to know where we come from and where we're going, otherwise we're lost puppies...

...And before he pushed his cart any further, he thought about how humans really have such a simple-minded view of anything and everything. He thought about love and how what is called love is probably something very different; he thought about what he really was to his wife and kids – a snoring breadwinner with an insatiable cock for the one and a big creature who liked to joke around and go to the park and buy ice cream and who wasn't around as much as Mommy for the others; he thought about how his life had been on a train track, for better or for worse, and how he hadn't been able to see himself getting off that track for at least another ten years while the kids got through college, though he had more and more regularly seen himself flying over the track and watching from above. He'd decided to put what he believed about life in parentheses for a while and live – albeit with the same people and places – outside of his usual parameters.

Anyway, when the flood hit, Bill was spared, but he never saw his wife and kids again. His wife, he knew, was a goner because he had watched her float away, face down, from his outstretched hand. His kids – one was finishing high school and the other starting college – had simply disappeared and, for all he knew, might have used the flood as a way to get away from Mom and Pops and start up their own lives.

The pull now, Bill felt as he walked the sidewalk in his dapper dark blue outfit, was hunger. Betty had given him a beer and some potato chips, but that was all he'd eaten since breakfast. He pulled the handle of the door to his friend Billy B's greasy spoon and went in with his mind set and his tongue licking the inside of his cheeks at the thought of a hamburger with everything on it. Billy B cut a thick slice of onion. Billy B's lettuce was fresh. Billy B's tomatoes were juicy and his fries were thick. The mustard, ketchup, pickle relish, and mayo were at your beck and call on the table.

"Just saw Betty Swain. She didn't want fifty bucks. Said it was too much. I told her she deserved a thousand, but us useless cops don't make enough to pay what people deserve for their work."

"Then pay me the extra for that hamburger you're salivating about. When you walk in the door I can tell what you want."

"You can just tell by the time of day."

"You might be right. So what do you want to drink with that Billy B burger?"

"Ice tea with a lot of ice. I just walked four blocks thinking about my miserable stomach and I need to cool it off."

"Any crime in this city yet, Bill?"

"Not that I know of."

"I wish my old buddies, Sully and Fireball Fred, had lived to see this."

"When'd they die?"

"Fred went three years before the flood and Sully kicked the damn bucket just a few months before. Sad he didn't get to see the kingdom of heaven on earth. He would have laughed his ass off when he saw who survived and who didn't."

"How old was he?"

"About seventy-five. The son of a bitch never really got old. He just dropped dead walking home one night. Fireball Fred died right next to where you're sitting. He had a heart attack during a Christmas party he and Sully organised. This gorgeous, bleached blonde with blessed bust-you-in-the-face boobies was sitting on his lap while he was playing Santa Claus. He fell over dead. Didn't even have time to say goodbye. Imagine that, my two best friends dropping like bowling pins without of a word of farewell."

"Would you have wanted it any other way?"

"Of course not. The blonde still lives in the neighbourhood. She's from Russia or Moldovia or something like that. She comes in every now and then. Sully met her on a bench in the park."

"I don't think Moldovia is – or was – a country, Billy."

"Well it don't matter now since the flood."

"Well, I'm glad you and your grease spot here survived."

"I count my ginger fucking blessings every day Bill. And I'm glad you moved to town."

"I told you, Billy, I didn't move here, I floated."

"I forgot."

"Would you please get to work on that hamburger before I hit you on the head with my nightstick."

"You don't have a nightstick."

"You bet I do. Just ask Betty Swain."

The door swung open and, lo and behold, in walked Olga, the bleached blonde with the sunshine chest and a lipsticked smile that looked like it was battery powered.

"Well, how are you Olga? We were just talking about you. About you and Sully and Fireball Fred. This is Bill the policeman. Bill, Olga."

"Nice to meet you Bill policeman. I haven't seen police around in a coon's age. They used to be on every corner like stop lights."

"The pleasure is mine, Olga."

"You know I used to have to run away from police back before the flood because I was bad girl all around, illegal alien.... Was that the word...? Alien? Sounds like some creature from space out...out space...and on top of that I was prostitute to make the ends meet."

"Well Olga, the flood did you a double favour: no more passports and borders and your profession has finally got the recognition it deserves. In fact I saw Betty Swain myself this afternoon on my lunch break. Do you know her?"

"Not that I know." Olga had taken a seat on a counter stool and with a cross-legged swivel was facing Bill who had edged towards the edge on the bench of the front booth. "She good?"

"Good as an eighty-year-old can be."

"She must be good if she work at eighty."

"She only took it up after her husband died. She was seventy-something."

Billy B had thrown on the meat for the hamburger and asked Olga what she wanted. "I like one pastrami with that hot mustard and one small beer." Since the flood Billy B could sell beer and basically anything else he wanted to as long as it wasn't poisonous. He quickly put the beer in front of Olga and she licked the head off it with one slow swipe. Bill the policeman got the automatic bubbled swirl in the gut. Every woman he ever met was immediately charted into one of two categories: the ones he would like to make love with and the ones he would not. He never told anybody this and he never wanted to hurt anyone's feelings. But it was true. The whole female population was bipolar, dichotomous, split like a log...those that turned on the jukebox and those that left it silent. Of course it was possible for a woman to change categories as time logged on, but regardless, they were always slotted on Olga's side or the other side of the dotted line.

"Nice day we're having," he finally said feeling the tip of his nose twitch like a bee wing.

"Summer coming," Olga said. "No clothes have to be on. You know what I mean. That was one of the reasons I come to America. Too cold where I come from. Too many clothes. Stupid living where clothes have to be like bear rugs."

"We do get our winters here."

"I know. I almost leave to go souther, but then flood came and I have to get organised again, and anyway, weather seems better now."

"Less clothes."

"You say it."

Bill invited Olga to join him at the table, which she did with the ado of a monkey changing branches. He got his burger. She got her pastrami. He got her calf on the inside of his knee just like he'd hoped for.

10

Yes, that's right. No more countries and no more passports. After the flood there were so few people left and so much to be done to get the world back on its feet, that the whole idea of keeping to borders became ludicrous. Everybody was needed and most everybody who survived pitched in to try to get things functioning again. Houses and hospitals had to be rebuilt; roads had to be repaired; airports and airplanes had to be put back in service; agriculture was turned topsy-turvy; people had to be found who had competences in fields where needs were most pressing; schools were not schools like before, but people were quickly trained to do something that was needed; children were working as soon as they could; tv streaming lost most of its clout because people didn't have time to sit on their butts all day; the whole advertising industry ceased to exist, as did Hollywood and professional and college sports – there was no time and nobody to watch; laws were rather simple in that no survivor was the kind of person who would take somebody else's stuff; courts were essentially useless, for the first few years at least; armies were out given that countries were out; the whole idea of a police force was put on hold for the first year as nothing was stolen and no one was murdered or attacked.

It took about two years to get the world functioning again. I enjoyed watching. (Yes, I know...But, unlike you, I really didn't have anything else to do.) I had always thought that it would take an invasion from outer space to bring the human race together. Well, the flood had the same effect. And given that the survivors did not believe in an afterlife, they worked their tails off to make this life worth living.

When the waters finally diminished, there were skeletons of cities and towns left. It was interesting to see how certain things were converted into other things. For example: football and baseball stadiums became pastures for cows and sheep; most shopping malls had a tendency to remain standing and most were turned into very nice and spacious apartment complexes; a few restaurants remained, but there were so many of them before the flood that those that were left standing were either torn down or converted into learning centres; most churches, it was decided by those who took power, were transformed into concert halls, but some were left in their original state as museums and landmarks of a past age.

One interesting thing that the survivors did was to rapidly put in place a programme for taking care of the many orphaned children. Children were a huge priority in that their potential for work was needed as soon as possible and it was naturally very important that they didn't grow up to want to take other people's stuff. Their care and "education" was an enormous task and to do it without the axes of the devil, hellfire, and damnation hanging over their lovely necks was a trick that most civilisations heretofore had not accomplished. A premium was finally put on a respect for this life and only this life because no adult believed in any other. Children were taught that simply being there was an unbelievable miracle for everybody and everything and that everything was to be treated with as much grace and care as possible. It reminded me of some of the things the so-called "Indians" of North America had taught before they were wiped out by the Christians moving westward. Similar things had been taught in many parts of Asia too.

When I watched all this happen, I have to admit that I didn't regret the flood. It was tough to see billions go, but really, things had become a rather intolerable mess.

11

Trains had gotten the upper hand on cars, though cars continued to move people from one place to another, but now without all the hoopla of leather seats, turbo engines, and sexy shells. People didn't care about that anymore. And since advertising didn't exist as an industry, there was no competition for the souls of car owners. Anything that ran was a good car.

Jay Papp, Philip's youngest, decided to take the train when he came north with his girlfriend to visit his father. They were sitting in the last seat of the last car watching the world whiz by with one eye and looking for each other's lips with the other. They were newly-mets and, since their first encounter in a laundromat two months prior, nothing had obtunded their initial sizzling hots for each other. They were in the throes of what is commonly referred to as "love at first sight". How long that love lasts is another issue, but here they were in the gaga stage. Neither had enough hands, lips, or genitalia. The body parts could have doubled just about everywhere and they would have known how to put it all to good use.

Her name was Violetta Poole and yes, she was sixteen. This bothered absolutely nobody because since the flood it was noncensoriously appreciated that the female body was in optimum condition at about fifteen or sixteen. Of course, people still respected the body as it gently but surely began and then ran its inevitable retrograde course – as attested to by Betty Swain's lucrative business and the mild, sporadic pulling power of Philip Papp's window undressing. But Violetta was Aphrodite, and now there was nothing in society to corrupt her and turn her into a teenage snot who thought she was the hottest piece of shit ever to burn up the People page in a newspaper. There were no "people pages". There were no Kim Kardashians or Jennifer Lopezes. But there were girls like Violetta and there were even more Jay Papps who appreciated the floriferous splendour of the female being.

That last seat in the train was the best seat anybody ever had. Jay had both enjoyed and endured a throbbing boner for the first hour of the trip until Violetta removed her blossomy spring jacket, spread it over her leg and Jay's midsection and, with the delicacy and dexterity of an old spinster threading a needle, fingered his fiery cock until relief came. She didn't care that her spring jacket had taken on a new, temporary, semi-transparent Pollocky design and a starchy consistency in the middle of its back.

They arrived north in the early evening and Philip Papp met them at the station. He was standing in the middle of the platform. They, exiting last from the last car, could be seen ambling slowly arm in arm, their outside hands dangling bags partially inflated by their stuff. Both had packed lightly for their four-day stay.

"Hi Dad. This is Violetta. Violetta, this is my father," Jay said proud of both of them. Violetta extended her right hand and Philip Papp took it in both of his and held it like French presidents in days of yore held the hand of a visiting First Lady.

"It's a pleasure to meet you, Violetta. Jay's told me so much about you."

"Me too. I mean about you."

"Are you two hungry? Would you like a bite to eat before we head home?"

"Yeah, I would. What about you Violetta?"

"I'd love something."

"Let's go over to Billy B's then. It's only a short walk from here. Let me take your bag, Violetta."

"Thank you, sir."

"You can call me Philip. Everybody else does except my children."

"Not Mr. Papp?" Violetta said politely.

"No, Philip is fine...Philip is fine."

The two men flanked Violetta and they walked through the main hall and out into the street. Cities were not what they used to be, of course. They had somewhat taken on the air of an amusement park at earliest opening or latest closing time when only a few people stroll rather aimlessly amid the sleeping attractions. Cities were no longer noisy or vibrant and people hurried towards very little. There had been so much work to do after the flood and so few people to do it. The survivors had been like veteran janitors, taking their time at everything but, with great effectiveness, getting done what needed to be scrubbed, vacuumed, arranged or washed. In all cities now, almost three years after the flood, there were the necessities of the life that used to be. Hospitals did their best to take away pain and keep limbs and organs functioning; a few lonely buses and taxis moved people from place to place; cars, though much rarer than in bygone days, puttered around much like in the early 1930s; grocery stores provided food, however the choice was now much restricted (where before there were two hundred different kinds of cold cereal or thirty kinds of ketchup, now there were only two or three of each); electricity kept lights on and machines operational; a clothing store could be found here and there; barber shops and beauty salons had slowly resurfaced, though, much like during the pre-flood pandemics, people had realised that they could cut their own hair rather easily and with no charge to anybody; a restaurant could be found every couple of blocks; schools were essentially training centres to teach people to do something that was needed to keep people housed, alive, and comfortable; sewers and toilet facilities had taken time to re-establish their incredible pre-flood efficiency; phones and computers linked people, but many people had little time to use them and far fewer people to communicate with than before. Interestingly, the whole entertainment world had not resurfaced at all. Firstly, people had had to work so much (rather like nineteenth-century pioneers) and had been too tired to care about being amused by repetitive, delightfully vacuous trash, but, secondly, most of the people who had created the stuff were coveters and were no longer around to produce and peddle their junk. Much had been destroyed and nothing was in the making. No television game shows, no family comedies, no shoot-'em-up-car-chasing-fire-balling-exploding-death-and-blood-every-where movies, no police intrigues because there was no crime and nobody cared about the old ones, no sports on TV because there were no leagues of anything (a few joggers were starting to reappear, but as most people worked and walked enough and didn't over-eat it was a rather superfluous activity; a few children could be seen throwing balls around and kicking cans or rocks, but the pre-flood obsession with the ball – baseball, football, soccer ball, basketball, tennis ball, and golf ball – had completely disappeared), no computer games had been resurrected or created, and movie houses had yet to be put back into operation. It seemed that the survivors, not believing in an afterlife, had little or no interest in watching other people do things, but rather preferred to do things themselves. *Do it, while you can* was the unspoken mantra of people on earth.

"Billy B's is right around this corner," Philip Papp said pointing with his free hand and lightly brushing Violetta's shoulder with his elbow. "They have wonderful hamburgers and fries. And Billy B's apple pie is up there with my grandmother's."

"Good Dad. Is this Billy B a friend?"

"A little bit. I started going there a few weeks ago. Bill the policeman recommended it. And he's right, it's good."

Philip pulled the door and they snuggled into a booth near the window. Billy B brought the menus over and said, "Well, you folks are lucky I stay open a little longer since the flood. I used to just do breakfast and lunch and get the hell out of here by four in the afternoon. But now, with so few restaurants, I need to stay open longer. I don't mind really. This is what I do best, so I might as well do it until my bucket gets kicked over."

"Billy, this is my son Jay and his girlfriend Violetta."

"The pleasure is mine I'm sure," Billy B said with a nostalgically horny, unaggressive smile. "You just in town to see the old man?"

"Yeah, I haven't been home for a year and I wanted Dad to meet Violetta."

"Well I'm sure Dad's happy to see you and meet Violetta. What can I get you to drink?"

Philip ran his tongue across his lower lip and waited for the younger ones to speak. "I'd like anything cold with no bubbles," Violetta said.

"Apple juice?"

"That's fine."

"And I'll have a beer," Jay said.

"Philip?"

"Oh, how about a glass of red wine?"

"Only got one kind. That California merlot. Remember the flood was hard on the vineyards. Not nearly as rough on the beer guys. So have a look at the menu and I'll be right back with the drinks."

Billy B did it all most of the time. He had a waitress come in once in a while when he was tired, but the place was small and he liked the variety of doing everything himself. Customers knew that if the restaurant was crowded they might have to wait a while, but people weren't in a hurry and eating had become something to be savoured and appreciated rather than of a case of stuffing sugary and salty mono-tasting chunks into the gullet with finger-pinched robotic hands, thoughtlessly.

"So Violetta, what do you do?" Philip asked without needing to look at the menu.

"I'm training and working in a hospital where old people decide when and how they want to die. It's pretty interesting because you see how one day or even one hour can mean so much to somebody. When they choose their own moment to die, time takes on a whole different aura...I think that's the word for it. I mean when you look into the eyes of somebody who has decided to die tomorrow at four o'clock, those eyes are telling you something. I like it. It's sad, but I like it."

"Where did you and Jay meet?"

"In a laundromat. My parents still don't have a washing machine. Neither does Jay. We were watching our clothes dry, going round and round in the dryer, and I was watching Jay watch me when he wasn't watching the dryer. He was watching me watch him, too, and the next thing you know we're talking and the next thing after that we're in love." She smiled at Philip then went back to reading the menu.

"I'll have the pastrami sandwich," Jay said.

"I'll have the special Billy B hamburger. And some french fries. You say they're good?"

"They really are," Philip said grinning at this young girl like she was on the menu. Under her flowery spring jacket (the only one she had) with the comely come stain on the back, she was wearing a white cotton blouse with the two top buttons tastefully unbuttoned. Everything seemed to float, including Philip's eyes. "I think I'll just have a salad," he said seeing his son's girlfriend's face gleam under the overhead lamp like an apricot in a Santa Monica sunset.

The door opened and in walked Olga and a tall man just leaning past middle age with an unkempt mane, rather large corduroy trousers, and an azure blue t-shirt with a basketball printed on it. They sat down at the table next to the Papp clan. Billy B puttered over with the drinks and, setting them down, said, "Olga, my darling, I haven't seen you for days. My eyes were beginning to hurt. Who's your friend?"

"This is Larry, Larry Farley. He just move to town. He come from out west. He have kids here and he want to be a little closer."

"Welcome to the wild, wild east. I'm Billy B," Billy said.

"Olga's the perfect person to show you around. She's got more friends than a swimming pool in the Mojave desert."

"She's done quite well so far. I've just been here a week."

"What are you doing or going to do here other than check on the kids?"

"That's a good question, Billy," Larry Farley said. "I've been a rather useless person since the flood. Pretty useless before as a matter of fact. I was a philosophy teacher, but we're a superfluous species these days."

"Depends on what you have to say," Philip Papp said behind him. "Once we get the world completely back on track, I'm sure that questions other than survival will make a comeback."

"Actually, I was semi-retired before the flood because I had run out of things to say and people had stopped listening anyway. There was so much crap in the air that everything had been watered down to Kool-Aid. The only philosophers anybody was listening to were Kanye West, Ricky Gervais, and Elsa from Frozen. Here that is. I can't vouch for the rest of the world, but I imagine it wasn't much different in Paris, Prague, or Pattaya."

"You talk philosophy with me last night," Olga said with a wink and a smile.

"I did? What did I say?" Larry said.

"You say that you think in another two thousand years people will be back to where they were before the flood. You say you think all the shit start over again and nobody will see this life for what it is...what you say?...a purring smoke puff in the idiot's imagination."

"Did I say all that? I must have been talking in my sleep."

"Olga, you're really taking care of Mr... Mr... What was your name again?" Billy B barked as he took menus off the Papp table and handed them to Larry and Olga.

"Farley. Larry Farley."

"You just jealous Billy B. I tell you years ago I trade you me for a dozen cheeseburgers any day. You never take me up on deal."

"I'm a bad businessman. Otherwise I'd have been retired long before the flood."

Farley turned to the table behind him and asked, "Are you all from around here?" He looked past Philip's head and caught a glance at Jay and Violetta stuck next to each other across the table.

"I live here, but my son Jay and his girlfriend are just up visiting from down south."

"Well, north, south, east, west, it all depends on where one's sitting," Larry said.

"See," Olga chirped, "you still talk philosophy."

"I guess one is a prisoner of who one is. What do you do Mr... Mr...?"

"Papp. I'm a bit like you. I'm having trouble making myself useful since the flood. I used to sell insurance, but now I put in toilets around town. But most of the toilets are now in, so I'm probably going to start doing something else. I might go into the cow business."

"You what?" Jay said.

"I might start raising cows for Billy B burgers."

"When did you get that idea?" his son said.

"Yesterday, watching myself eat in here. I was holding my hamburger and looking at the juice drip out, and I thought that whoever raises these cows is a helluva nice guy."

"That's the beauty of the flood," Farley piped in. "Everybody appreciates each other now. And nobody's trying to cash in on anything, cows included. People are just trying to help each other get by. A good hamburger is part of getting by."

"You still talking in sleep," Olga said, sliding her long shiny-nailed fingers under the table and pawing at Farley's quiet crotch like one of those three-pronged cranes dipping after a pitiful stuffed animal for fifty cents in a family restaurant waiting room before the flood. She got the animal and Farley's head jerked a few degrees clockwise. "What we eating?"

"HAM-burger..."

"Okay, hamburgers. Two, Billy B."

Before they started eating Olga told Philip to be sure to treat those cows nicely before he ground them up and to be sure that cows with balls were made not to suffer when they got de-balled, at which point her hand below the table squeezed, Violetta winced, and the ex-philosophy teacher felt his jaw lock, his eyes blink, and a calm string of seconds pass until the flicker that preludes the smooth construction of the miniature high-rise.

12

Again, I don't regret the flood. If nothing else it made all necessary jobs equally important. One of the things I had hated most on the pre-flood planet was how most cultures gave more status to one job over another. A street sweeper was a nobody and a doctor was hot tuna. Both jobs were necessary to the civilisation and yet one was looked down upon and the other glorified. What idiocy! Cleaning toilets was seen as a degrading activity, whereas acting in Hollywood films was perceived to be noble. If anything, the opposite should have been true. Lawyers had status, bus drivers didn't. How ludicrous, how primitive, how lacking in imagination! The social totem pole was not a sign of intelligence, but the contrary thereof. To imagine that a garbage collector was not proud of his job in the same way that a judge or a senator was to reveal that the earth, before the flood, was the home of a lame, broken, cretinous society. When the waters took people away, those that remained and had to put things back together again were also those who realised that every useful job was as important and worthy as the next.

How and why people had come to be what they were is a fruitless question whose answer, like the answer to the inquiry "Why something and not nothing?", will never be known. I just know that I was tired of what I was seeing and what's crawling around now is easier for me to digest than what was there three little years ago.

13

"You beast, you. You dirty filthy lovely beast."

"That's the nicest thing anybody has said to me in years. If I may, I return the compliment."

"Look at your knees. They bleeding."

"Your carpet's at fault."

"Your knees not tough."

"Not enough work."

"You call this work?"

"I forgot who's paying who."

"Don't forget or I throw you out with next garbage bag."

"Do you supply Band-Aids for the knees?"

"No, I lick them. My lick cures many maladies."

"That'll do. But you'd better hurry before I bloody your carpet."

"I'm not blind. I can see blood roll."

"It isn't rolling, it's running."

"It rolls under microscope. Remember I was doctor before in my country."

"Your country no more country. Remember we all one big happy family now."

"You sound like me."

"You filthy dirty lovely animal."

"How long you plan to stay?"

"That depends on the stock market."

"There no more stock market."

"Then it depends on love."

"And what does love depend on?"

"Filthy dirty lovely animals like you."

She did lick both knees. He stayed for a total of thirty-three orgasms. At an average of three a day, you do the math. It had been a dry spell. Olga didn't need to be told. She knew how to bring life to the arid land.

14

Every time Philip Papp looked at Violetta Poole he ached. She was polite, she was beautiful, she was respectful, she was as sexy as a mermaid, she was as sweet as sugary sixteen can be. And she was his son's girlfriend. I watched it all. I've watched it a million times before. In fact, when I get bored, one of the things I enjoy watching most is how older men deal with the excitement younger women inspire. Excitement right in the gut, in the joint, in the heart of hearts, in the loins, in the shrunken prick that hasn't forgotten what it's like to drill the depths of luscious pussy.

Poor Philip Papp had Jay and Violetta around him for four days. On the morning of the third day he wrote a short letter to his son. While Violetta was showering after a wake-up multiple orgasm, Philip gently knocked on his son's door. When Jay opened it, his father handed him the letter and turned and walked back to the kitchen.

Dear son,
Could you, would you, lend me Violetta for just two hours?
She would do me a world of good.
Love, Dad

Jay read the note as he ambled from the door to the bed in his baby-blue boxer shorts: *could you, would you lend me Violetta for just two hours...?*

Of course he couldn't. But he could, for once, see his father in a different light, from a different angle. No anger, no pity, no emotion really, just a raw glimpse at a raw longing, the world a wishing place and his own father leading the charge of the great cavalry of men trying to find a way to deal with their mickle mucky juices. Maybe all of man's wars had been just that: a way to bury juice, to take it off the earth's face and hide it under a few feet of ground, to occupy the great masses of men, to throw them into beastly battle where copulation was temporarily wiped from the collective mind...

Violetta came out of the bathroom as naked as a spider. Jay had refolded the letter and let it drop unnoticed to the floor while Violetta was drying her hair. He gave it a soft kick and it floated under the bed where he would later retrieve it and dispose of it. He wanted no one else to see his father's bare soul, especially Violetta.

When she finished drying her hair she came toward the bed where Jay had lain, his hands behind his head, his knuckles in the pillow, to watch his girlfriend do nothing but change her body weight from one leg to the other as she dabbed the towel into her mahogany mane. She saw he had a hard-on which was enough to juice her and she pulled down his shorts and sat on it.

Jay Papp never said a word to his father about the letter and Philip Papp never mentioned it either. At the end of the fourth day, Jay and Violetta walked alone to the station and boarded the silver steel train heading south.

15

You might be wondering who was running the show. Governmentally, that is. The flood did away with every existing political system. It also, as I said, did away with national borders and, at least temporarily, all chauvinistic tendencies. Without gods and covetous desires, the survivors were, overall, a very tolerant open people. And surviving survival was on everybody's mind. People everywhere realised that everybody had to work together to bring back a semblance of civilisation. And people working together everywhere required a common form of communication. The flood had left herds of people hundreds, even thousands, of miles from their homes where their native language wasn't spoken. It didn't take long for everybody to figure out that English was the only chance for the human race to talk collectively and for English to get itself unofficially crowned, excuse the defunct verb, as the planetary language. Most people had some notion of it anyway, and those who didn't, like one-year-old kids thrown into the family babble, picked it up rather quickly. Love and necessity are the best motivation for learning a new language. Necessity put English on top.

So who was governing whom and with what kind of political system or systems?

Immediately after the flood, as can easily be imagined, chaos reigned. The flood was not a local affair where the unflooded could come in and help the flooded. No, everybody got soaked. But not everybody drowned. When the waters finally subsided all the survivors could rightfully be called "wanderers". Everybody was dazed and everybody was wandering around trying to figure out where they were and wondering if they might meet somebody they knew who was alive. The dead were a kind of universal debris, but so too were what had been the everyday objects of a collective human consciousness – strewn about in water and mud like ashes in a sea where a fleet of giant cruise ships had exploded. Nothing was in its normal place and nothing functioned. Books and newspapers floated about lithely like dead flatfish, street signs had turned into skinny rafts, maps were nowhere to be found, electricity and telephone lines were everywhere down and lying about in mangled piles, no phones were working, nor computers, nor televisions, nor radios; there was no music or cars or trucks or planes or trains or honking horns; the only travelling sounds were from water lapping the sides of thousands of makeshift boats. For a couple of months the world was in a sense an Eden, albeit a deconstructed one. There was a kind of pristine peace; in every direction that an eye turned water glistened and all the rest seemed to be afloat. The surviving Adams and Eves and their children wandered until they found their original homes (most never did) or somewhere their lives might begin afresh. Many families were – "miraculously" one is tempted to say – able to find each other and stay together, but far more were cut to pieces by raging water and death.

It took two of these idyllic months before the flood water completely seeped back into the earth and people were starting to sleep in places they could weakly refer to as "home". Enough houses and buildings had been left standing such that there was essentially no construction that was needed to be done. Things just had to be repaired and cleaned up, and people had to find a nest to call their own. All of this did take some leadership, of course. If two people wanted to settle in the same place somebody had to make a decision. And somebody had to organise the cleaning, the repair crews, and the disposal of a few billion bodies.

So who grabbed the power in this new beginning? Not surprisingly, people who had had it before the flood. People who were used to making decisions for a group started making them again... "Okay, you take this place, and you...what was your name?... Yes you, Juan, take that place over there. You said you had a husband with you and a child? Yes, then you take that place over there... And how about if the five of you find some shovels and start cleaning the mud out of this building... And you, you four...do you feel okay?... See if you can move those cars away from that house..."

Given that the survivors were only people who didn't covet other people's goods and lives, the whole process of getting people housed went very smoothly. Groups of people formed all over the wet globe and leaders quietly started stepping forward everywhere. These first leaders were not selected but arose naturally as in any situation where power has been momentarily vacuumed away.

Little by little life found a grain of normalcy, but a normalcy far removed from the pre-flood world of three hundred TV stations for a house with five people and five TVs, traffic jams, supermarkets, mega-everything stores, airplanes jamming runways and skies, zillions of emails and voicemails, Putin, Trump, Harry & Meghan, tourism, nine-to-fiveism, two car garagism, vacations to a sunny beachism, the richism and the poorism, high taxism,

Brexitism, Africanism, the wars in Afganistanism and Iraqism, cyber wafareism, the simmering war between certain adherents of Christianism and Islamism, trying to keep up with the Jonesesism, fast foodism, rappism music, technoism music, gay paradeism, Thanksgiving paradeism, communism, neo-nazism, capitalism, insurance companyism, hospitals making huge profitsism, insurance companies making obscene profitsism, anybody making a profitism, sports teamsism, sports leaguesism, sports commentatorsism, political commentatorsism, right-wingism, left-wingism, centrism, born-again Christianism, radio call-in showsism, unborn-again Christianism, Hinduism, Buddhism, Taoism, Shintoism, Mormonism, Catholicism, baptistism, evangelism, bigotism (bigots always wanted other people's shit), used car dealersism, top modelism, Heisman trophyism, Hollywoodism, schoolism, Harvardism, Yaleism, Eton Cronyism, Arizona Stateism, kindergartenism, day careism, who caresism?, nobody caresism... Hey, you name it...it almost certainly wasn't around.

Yes, the flood did what it was intended to do: it gave the world a new start.

So after nearly three years, what did politics look like?

About six months after the flood, communication systems were functioning. Enough technicians had survived to get phone masts and satellites communicating and the internet back on the screen. The world was starting to interact with itself again. A few roads had opened up and a few cars and buses were moving people around. Trucks were more visible because they were doing so much hauling of debris. After eight months, the first airplane was back in the air, a flight from Singapore to Bangkok had a few hundred exhausted onlookers clapping their dirty-fingernailed hands.

Clusters of people, primarily in and around what had been large metropolitan areas, were starting to call themselves names like "New Parisians", "New New Yorkers" or "New Tokyo-yos". Most said so jokingly, it didn't stick. But slowly and surely, semi-stable leaders of these geographic clusters were needed and there was a concomitant need for a group to be represented by somebody to talk about issues that concerned other groups: a hospital was functioning again and could the people from another cluster use it? who puts back up the street signs and for what areas? who teaches whom how to weld a broken beam? how much time should people work a day? should all food be pooled together for common meals in common areas? who cleans whose water? who fixes whose pumps? should bartering stop and should money be brought back into circulation? who should control any eventual money? who should coordinate the effort of separated family members trying to find each other? who cultivates which fields? who distributes what to whom?

On and on went the reasons to put people in place to make decisions. With communication systems back on their toes local leaders began to talk among each other. One thing became evident as people started talking around: though there was a certain appreciation for how complicated and amazing the world had been before the flood, nobody wanted to reproduce that same world. Nobody wanted the world of 1975 or 1989 or 2000 or 2022. What the "new" world would be was hard to tell, but there was a consensus about clearing the table of tons of crap.

So cluster leaders communicated. As a result, the globe being big and all, newspapers, streaming, social media and podcasts started to reappear. The great internet once again became a kind of frosting on the communal cake. In other words, some crap could do nothing other than litter the table again. As a means to an equitable end.

But what were people saying? Who was doing ye olde tweeting now?

Remember, there were no believers and no coveters. Not yet anyway.

The first major decision was the need for an interactive world government. Nobody wanted to go back to separate "countries" or nation-states. "We're all in this mess together" was the new prevailing feeling; new to the west at least. No more let-the-Africans-die-down-there-wherever-the-hell-they-are-in-their-corner-of-famine-and-AIDS-and-whatever-the-hell-civil-war-is-killing-them-off-like-flies. No, this time it'll be different. We'll work together. There aren't that many of us. We need each other. We've got fucking world communication, so let's use it. And in this world let's let people live wherever the hell they want to live. Let the "people" market take care of itself. Nobody should be forced to live in any part of the world. No more refugees. No more asylum. No more green or blue or brown passports to be shown at history's ever-changing imbecilic borders.

The second major decision was to clean up the mindset of the workforce. Gone were the millionaire lawyers and doctors and the ten-dollar-an-hour street sweepers. No, street sweepers are as necessary as doctors to a civilised society. Every necessary job gets the same status and same pay, no matter what we decide to pay with. Everybody who's doing something useful counts...

And yes, we will need a world currency. Money is a necessary evil. (With no gods, do "good" and "evil" mean anything...? These kinds of questions started sprouting up a little later.) Money in itself isn't bad; it's kind of fun to jingle a little change in your pocket...

Healthcare should be the same for everybody. Only an insane world gives wonderful care to some people and lets others rot in their own stinking misery.

Transportation should absolutely not be a dangerous operation. Nobody should get killed going from here to there. We've got to get rid of road accidents. During the duration of the Vietnam war more people died on the roads of France than American soldiers on the battlefield. That kind of insanity must not be allowed to come back.

And animals...ah animals...what should we do about animals? Should we continue to eat them? Should we let them roam? Should we elevate their status? Chickens and pigs were still being eaten rather regularly, but for whatever reason, people were starting to rethink the cosmological standing of cows. (Were a disproportionate number of survivors Hindus?) Steaks and hamburgers continued to appear on plates, but many people were starting to sense gentle mooing sounds echoing through their brains when they looked at menus or stood before a slice of beef at the butchers.

Time, it was finally decided after a few days of global discussion, would be counted differently. Out went "B.C." and "A.D." Since nobody believed in divinity, Jesus's birthday got thrown out as the start of the great clock-on-the-wall. It wasn't 2000 A.D. anymore; it was 24 B.F. A new clock was set in motion. B.F. and A.F. with the great deluge splicing the middle.

And on and on things went for those first few months.

There were no countries formed or reformed, though the old names were used by most – especially by older people – for the first couple decades, even if they meant nothing in practice. There was an initial skeleton of a world government in that clusters were communicating with each other all over and expressing what was going well and what was needed. Hospitals were for everybody. English was being learned everywhere, though dialects were still spoken. In only a few areas was power distributed through elections. For the most part leaders still rose naturally as on a children's playground or as with the Sioux or Navaho tribes of bygone days.

Interestingly, different parts of the world started prospering wherein before the flood there had been very little. Deserts were more fertile now and a lot of luscious forest had been ripped away. Many people had ended up at the foot of mountains and hence mountains, more than coastlines, tended to border human herds.

After two and a half years of getting things back into a liveable state, it was decided that every cluster of people would send two participants to a global conference that would take place six months later, in 3 A.F., in the place that used to be Geneva, Switzerland. The conference would try to set up a world government and establish some common rules for all of the living. Nobody bitched about the choice of location. The "Swiss" cluster had already set up a short string of smiling hotels and by 3 A.F would have enough rooms with beds to accommodate a few thousand participants. Everybody would have time to get there. The meeting was still a few months away.

16

In the meantime, Larry Farley went to work with Billy B. Billy decided he would start cutting his own hours – he was creeping up on seventy and the smoke and steam off the grill wasn't making him any younger – and essentially, he made Farley a partner in the greasy spoon. They would split profits (the dollar was back in use west of the Atlantic and east of Manila) after costs had been weeded out. Once Farley learned how to cook, he would work a few more hours a day than Billy because Billy was a dozen years older and had been cooking burgers and pastrami sandwiches for forty years. They would keep the restaurant open a little longer as demand was stretching the hands on the clock. There would be enough for both of them to live on. They quickly decided to take Olga on full time as a waitress. A couple of months prior she had expressed – to Farley one summer night in a park under a star-soaked sky – a growing sentiment that if possible she would just as soon start selling something else after fifteen years of peddling her curves, canyons, and melon-slice lips. Both men liked the idea of keeping Olga rather close at hand and they were sure she would be good for business.

She was.

Philip Papp and Bill the policeman were sitting together chewing on hamburgers when Philip Papp said, "Any of you guys see anything about this convention coming up in Switzerland? Looks like we're going to get ourselves a President of the World."

"Who the fuck wants a President of the World! It was bad enough having a President of the YOU-nited States!" Billy B howled from behind the grill.

"I don't know, but why else would they have a world convention?"

"I like the way things are now. I pay a whole lot less taxes since the flood."

"That's because there's a whole lot less people and crap to take care of."

"Well let's keep it that way."

Bill the policeman swallowed and said, "I read yesterday that each cluster group could send two representatives to the meeting. I think Farley ought to go for us. He's as full of shit as anybody I know. He'd be perfect. He's got nothing else to do but flip burgers all day."

"You wanna flip for a while?" Billy B said.

"I can't. I'm a cop."

"But you've got nothin' to do but sit in here and gobble all day."

"I won't argue."

"So why don't *you* go?"

"I can't talk like Farley. He had all that experience teaching college kids philosophy."

"It's true, he could talk his way out of a horse's ass."

"That's what I mean. Let's get him in there. Where is he anyway? And where's Olga?"

"Olga's off today and Farley's at the dentist's. He should have been here an hour ago."

"Why'd he go to the dentist?"

"Why does anybody go to the dentist – because we've got teeth. If we didn't have teeth we wouldn't have dentists. If we didn't have ears we wouldn't be talking. If we didn't have legs we wouldn't have wheelchairs. If sneezing took ten seconds instead of a half a second we wouldn't have cars. Can you imagine driving along at fifty miles an hour and going *AH—AHH—AHHH— AHHHHHH—CHOOOOOOOOOOOOOOOO* for ten seconds. You'd crash into something. What I mean is, everything's related."

"You've been talking to Farley too long."

"Probably."

"Hey Philip, I forgot to ask you. How's that son of yours handling that Lolita he was up here with?"

"He seems to be okay. He hasn't written or called much lately."

"She had to be one of the cutest girls I've ever seen."

"Who?" Farley said walking in the door.

"That girl Philip's son brought up here from deep down south."

"She made me want to believe in God," Farley said.

"Never thought of it that way," Bill the policeman said.

"Makes me want to cry," Billy B said. "What about you Philip? What did she make you want to do?"

Philip didn't – couldn't – say anything. His silence was rescued by Bill the policeman. "Anybody seen Betty Swain lately?"

"No, I haven't. Have you Larry?"

"I saw her two weeks ago, but not since then," Philip Papp said, happy to change the subject.

"That woman's an angel. There might be a heaven just for her."

"I haven't seen her for a month," Farley said. "Last time I saw her she was chatting under a tree with a woman and a young boy."

"That must have been Tamalia Lattner and her kid. Betty and Tammy have gotten to be good friends," Bill the policeman said.

"Speaking of good friends," Billy B said, "tell our good friend Larry here your idea about sending him to Switzerland for us."

"I was just telling Philip and Billy B that we should sign you up to go to that world convention they're having pretty soon."

"What world convention? I haven't read a newspaper in a month."

"The one in Switzerland. Every cluster gets to send two representatives."

"Who's idea was this?"

"How the hell should I know? What difference does it make? We decided you're our guy. We want you to go."

"Who's 'we'?"

"Me, Philip, and the King of the Grill," Bill the policeman said chortling.

"Who's gonna cook the burgers?" Farley shot back.

"I'll cook the burgers," Philip Papp said. "Like Bill says Larry, you could talk your way out of a horse's ass."

"I won't do it. I hate politics."

"Yes you will. You love politics. You always get what you want. That's good politics."

"Go chew on your hamburgers."

"Not until you say you'll do it."

"What makes you think the rest of our cluster will want me?"

"I've got connections," Bill said. "I'll be your campaign manager. I'll talk to the right people."

"What would I do without you guys?"

"What would we do without you? You're our spiritual leader."

"Olga's the only spiritual leader you guys know. The only time any of you look like you've got a fucking spirit is when she's prancing around this two-bit café and your eyes are bouncing off her ass like the balls in a pinball machine."

"Don't be so hard on us Larry. We're lonely men. We're past our primes. Our reproductive organs have marinated so long in their own juices that they risk dissolving into thin air," Billy the policeman said, cocking his head like he was about to fabricate a tear. "Please Larry, go to Switzerland for us. Help make a good world. It's only a convention. You'll be back with the fellas in no time."

"The truth is I haven't been over there since my honeymoon. All I remember is my wife wanting to jump in Lake Geneva because she thought I had the hots for the girl at the reception desk in our hotel."

"Did she jump?"

"No."

"Did you have the hots for the receptionist?"

"I needed somebody to have a honeymoon with."

"You're our guy, Larry. You'll be the next Bill Clinton."

"By the way, did Clinton survive the flood?"

"I think so."

"But he coveted a lot of wives."

"They were all already on the rocks with their husbands, so it didn't count."

"Who was it – I can't remember – that figured out that all of us sorry survivors didn't believe in God and weren't spending our time coveting other people's shit?"

"Who was it? Come on Philip. You don't remember that?"

"No, I don't."

"That was our man Farley, Larry Farley. It made world news." Bill the policeman stared around the room. Then, having no gavel, he slowly raised and then lowered his fist to the formica table. "That was our man Farley," he repeated.

"That is our man Farley," Philip Papp said with a nod and a slight bow of his head.

"I second the motion," Billy B said.

"Screw you all," Farley said.

17

One of the things that fascinates me most about you people is how you see time as extending only as far as your mortal eyes and hands can measure. What you see is what you get. What you can measure is all that you can imagine.

But you're blind, so very blind. You never imagine that things go back way beyond your millions and billions and trillions of years, as you call them. You watch your suns and your moons and your planets and you measure. But you're not measuring time. You're measuring your measure of time: a few piano heartbeats in the great vast creamy black silence of what you call the universe.

But that's all right. You can't do otherwise. I'm just surprised that more of your so-called thinkers don't spin that great clock-on-the-wall and go backwards and forwards so far that you can't see anymore. Then you will have made a good start.

But that's all right.
Who wants to get dizzy over such a matter?

18

The beauty of beauty is that it shows up when it is least expected. When you wait for a sunrise or sunset it usually doesn't produce the anticipated result. When somebody tells you that you've got to see this or that "because it's so beautiful", there is often a let-down when the solicited object finally comes before one's eyes.

No, the beauty of beauty is in the absence of forewarning.

Betty Swain and Tamilia Lattner were sitting in the park equidistant from their two places of residence. Chipper was swinging on a swing. Betty looked at Tammy and thought, Oh my God, what a beautiful mouth. They hadn't spoken for a couple of minutes. Tammy was looking in the direction of her son; her mouth was slightly open. Her lips were covered with a dark rose-coloured gloss that was neither too shiny nor not shiny enough. Betty was seated at an angle such that from the right corner of Tammy's mouth the outer lines rose and fell in perfect harmony. The upper part of the lower lip and the lower part of the upper lip were absolutely identical. Neither lip took control over the other. They were as symmetrical as a baby's rump and where the morning sun's light hit them they looked to be streaked with white gold.

"You know you have beautiful lips," Betty Swain said meaning it not to be a question.

"Thank you. They were not my making, but I do try to not mess them up."

"Did your husband appreciate them?" Betty asked.

"Could be, but he tended to be a little coarse around the edges. In the middle too for that matter."

"That's too bad."

"A lot of things are too bad. How are you feeling today?"

"Better, but I still don't feel up to working," Betty said softly.

"You've worked enough in your life. Let it be for now."

With her right hand Betty rubbed up the back of her thigh and Tammy watched the old woman's fingers open and close and pull at the loose flesh under the skirt.

"The way I feel now, I'll probably never work again. But my strength might come back. You never know.... My you have a beautiful mouth. I'd never noticed it before."

"We were too busy talking."

"Too busy makes the blind blinder."

"That's a good way to put it."

"Your husband died before the flood didn't he?"

"In 2015. About 9 B.F. as we say today. I doubt he would have survived anyway. He was always wanting what other people had.... Cars, house, tennis racket, shoes. Even kids. He used to say how much he'd like to have a daughter *like so-and-so's*. I'm sure he wanted other men's women too. For all I know he had some. But I never knew about anything and I never asked. I had Chipper to play with."

"Such a darling boy. I remember the first time I saw him. Polite and patient."

"Yes."

"I have wanted to talk to you about something, Tammy. It's what to do with me when I'm dead, if you know what I mean." Betty stopped rubbing her thigh and looked at Chipper on the swing, her head slightly bobbing as the boy did his half revolutions.

"You have no family, do you?"

"Not that I know of. Of course I might, but I wouldn't know where."

"Yes, I see."

"Really the only person I can think of is you. To tell you what I want done with me when I'm dead."

"I'll be happy to do whatever you'd like, Betty, but who knows, you might go on living for years and years."

"I don't think so. I can feel it coming and as it gets closer it comes more quickly, rather like a train you see way down the horizon that is heading your way."

"Since the flood I haven't had anyone die. No one I know that is. It's strange, before, funerals and things were always shrouded with a hint of life after this world. There was always a taste of a hereafter – like salt in soup – even for people like me who didn't believe in gods. But now I wonder what funerals are like. I haven't been to any since we buried all those billions."

"I went to one. One of my neighbours a couple years ago. He had asked for nothing except he wanted everybody in attendance to kiss him on the forehead. There was some music, then everyone walked by and kissed him like he'd asked. There were a couple dozen of us. The whole thing only took about fifteen minutes. I don't know where they buried him. I kissed him and walked straight home."

"Who did the ceremony?"

"A man named Gus. He introduced himself, put on the music, then when the music finished, he opened the coffin and explained what my neighbour wanted. He kissed him first."

"Yes."

"Well, I've been thinking. I'd like just one thing myself. I'd like a group of twelve or so small children – ages maybe six or seven to nine – to hold hands in a circle around my coffin and sing a song or two. That's all."

"What songs would you like?"

"That's what I wanted to ask you about. And I want you to get the children and teach them the songs. Of course, I want Chipper to sing."

"Of course. I'd be happy to do anything for you, Betty." Tamilia put her arm around Betty. Betty was still staring at Chipper on the swing.

"I know I want one song for sure."

"Yes?"

"I want 'Happy Birthday', but instead of saying 'happy birthday', I want the kids to say 'happy deathday'... *Happy deathday to you / Happy deathday to you / Happy deathday dear Be-tty / Happy deathday to you....*"

"That's a beautiful idea."

"But I'd like maybe one other song. Can you think of one?"

"Would you like a children's song?"

"Yes."

Tammy thought for three blinks of an eye. "I know. How about '*Row row row your boat / Gently down the stream / Merrily merrily merrily merrily / Life is but a dream...?*'"

"Perfect Tammy. I think that'll do. Just those two songs and then goodbye."

"Yes."

"You know, I've been thinking, too, that I'll choose the time of my own death. If there's one thing a person should be able to choose it's when to stop living. That's why I wanted to talk to you. Before it's too late. Before dying gets me, I want to get it. I'm quite ready to go."

"I'll only support you, Betty. You've been through a lot. You've helped a lot of people. You've given the world your joy. I've seen it. I just wish I'd met you earlier. It'll be an honour for me to help you."

Her head not moving, Betty closed her eyes and folded her hands in her lap. "Thank you Tammy," she said. "You know, it's amazing, but even with my eyes shut I can see your mouth. And Chipper on the swing. Your mouth; Chipper on the swing." She went silent, then said, "At least, sort of."

19

It was after Betty Swain left the park bench and went home that Tamilia Lattner met Larry Farley for the first time. She had stayed on into the morning, content to be warm on a bench in the spring sun while her boy went from swing to jungle gym to slide to rocking horse to tunnel, on and on, as if it were his first time for all of them. She had brought a book, *The Remains of the Day* – in the eventuality that Betty's stay was shorter than hers – which she was now reading. The park had filled up considerably with children and parents, leaving little space on the few benches that allowed people to get off their feet and stay awhile. Larry Farley had stood behind the two rocking horses looking around. Tamilia, sitting to his left, saw him looking and realised he wasn't looking for a child, but for a place to sit. She caught his eye, gestured with the hand that held her book, and moved over a foot or so.

"Thank you," Farley said lowering his lanky frame, careful not to disturb the child's jacket and woman's sweater bundled together on the bench. "The place looked pretty much sold out."

"There's always room for one more. At least that's what my mother used to always say." Tammy smiled and turned her head about thirty degrees and almost looked at Farley.

"Must have been a nice mother."

"As a matter of fact she was. I never saw her angry, except one time when I wore a mini skirt to a high school dance. She cried, but when I came home that night – it must have been around midnight – she was still awake and asked me if I'd had fun. She never spoke about the skirt again...Then again, I didn't wear it too often after that."

"Did you have fun?"

"Don't remember a thing except my mother's crying."

"Is she still alive?"

"No, she isn't."

"Did she go with the flood?"

"That's the funny thing. She didn't. She went to church every Sunday for probably seventy years of her life. Her great grandparents had been Mormon pioneers. But, for whatever reason, the flood spared her."

"She must have gone to church for social reasons. Maybe she used the time she was sitting on those hard pews to wonder what the hell life was all about."

"She probably thought more about what meals she was going to cook the upcoming week. She was the most organised woman I've ever seen. But she never looked stressed or in a hurry. But you're probably right about the meaning of life stuff, too. After I found her after the flood – I'm pretty sure that only she and I survived from our family of eight – we were talking one day and she told me how deep down inside she had always thought that God and Santa Claus were the same person. Then she'd burst out laughing."

At this point Tammy and Farley were looking at each other while they talked. "There might have been quite a few like her," he said.

"Could be," she said.

"So when did she die?"

"A year and a half ago. At least she got to play with Chipper for a bit."

"Chipper her dog?"

"No, he's my son." She raised and pointed a finger toward the top of the jungle gym.

Farley smiled and followed her hand, tilted his head, and said, "Is that him in the blue shirt?"

"That's him. That's my boy, my one and only."

"His shirt is almost the same colour as the sky."

"I hadn't noticed even though I love the sky."

While she was looking at the sky he saw the lips. Then he saw the cheeks that were tastefully powdered and twinkled here and there. Her mouth was slightly open. "I think that's the first time I've ever heard anyone say they love the sky," he said now looking at her ear that had shiny brown hair pulled behind it.

"I've loved the sky since I was a little girl. It's always there one way or another. I love it no matter how it looks...grey, black, white, blue like Chipper's shirt...I figure that without the sky we'd be nowhere."

"Never thought of it that way."

"It's like a painting. If you take away the background, the rest of the picture is going to look stupid. The background gives it its sense. Same for the sky. At least that's what I think, anyway."

Larry Farley looked at the wide flat powdery blue eleven o'clock spring sky and couldn't disagree. "What do you do, if you don't mind my asking?"

"A lot of this. Watching Chipper. Sitting in parks. This one's my favourite. Not much otherwise. Before the flood I had been married and was teaching kindergarten until Chipper came along. My husband drowned, so it's me and Chipper."

"What are you reading?"

She held up the book. "The Remains of the Day. It's by a Japanese guy who is – or was – English actually. It's about two people in love who waste their lives by never getting together. I'm almost finished. It's good."

The man looked at the woman. There's something about her, he thought. There's something about everybody, he rethought, but there's something about this woman that's not about most other women. He couldn't quite figure out what it was. Then he wondered if she might think there was something about him, wondering if her side of the bench was also starting to feel warm. Then he wondered if when he was fascinated by a woman he was more fascinated by the feeling of fascination than by the woman herself.

"What do you do?" she asked, the words blowing past her lips as if Farley could see them.

"Actually I have a new job. The cluster group here just nominated me to go to the big world convention that's coming up in what used to be Switzerland. Otherwise I had been a philosophy teacher and more recently a cook in a rather delicious greasy spoon."

"Which did you like better, the philosophy or the greasy spoon?"

"Pretty much a tossup. Both have their ups and downs."

"That's what I like about raising Chipper. Almost no downs."

"I have two older children. I felt the same way."

"I've been following the newspapers about this convention. How did you get nominated?"

"I really don't know. Do you know Bill the policeman?"

"I've seen him around."

"It was his idea to begin with. He went to some meeting and talked some hearty trash about me and the next thing I know I'm nominated."

"When's the meeting?"

"In a month."

"Should be interesting."

"Actually the more I think about it the more I'm excited to go. Before the flood I left politics to the swirling winds of history. The machine was too big. There was no slowing it down. But now, maybe now – with this crew we have on the earth – something can be done."

"What kind of something would you like to do?"

"I'm still thinking. Have you got any ideas?"

"A few."

"What kind?"

"How to get people to love the sky."

And so it was that Larry Farley proposed to Tamilia Lattner that she go with him to the convention as the other cluster representative. She agreed and was unanimously approved by Bill the policeman and the nominating committee. Everybody liked the idea of a man and a woman and loving the sky.

Two weeks later Tamilia, Chipper, and Larry Farley were on a big boat crossing the ocean. They had two rooms with a door in between. The door was never opened, even after Chipper had gone to sleep.

20

To be honest, I had been looking forward to the convention for quite some time. Rather like a lot of you, in pre-flood days, used to look forward to a football game or a date on an operating table with a heart surgeon; I wanted to see what would happen.

Civilisation had bored me. There were some amusing moments, but when I look back, overall, grosso modo, what had humans done with their lives? A lot of gods, a lot of myths, a lot of law making, a lot of slavery, a lot of lies, a lot of trying to stay warm, a lot of screwing, a lot of families, a lot of crises, a lot of disease, a lot of time spent to keep the belly full, lately a lot of business, (I want to say a lot of love, but let's be honest – here's where the lies come in – most of what is called love is simply what makes one feel good), a lot of forgetting, a lot of dying (much of which was my responsibility), a lot of giving, a lot of motherly affection, and a lot of building, especially in the last decades B.F. with all the people that were around.

When I look back at this little slice of human time, a few cultures stick out. The Egyptians had their moments, with their cats and pyramids and queens and all. The Greeks weren't bad either, although Plato, a decent guy at heart, probably did more harm than good with his ideal forms and transcendental bullshit. The Romans were an amusing bunch for a while (I must admit that even to this day I have a soft spot for things Italian), but after they imploded there was a long, dark, dry spell. Fortunately the Renaissance came along to raise my spirits. China and Japan had some curious moments as well, but as often as not, they had me asleep on my couch. The Americas, the Aztecs, Incas, and particularly some of the more northern Native American tribes also were not without interest. But when they were shot down by their navigating conquerors, I must admit that boredom was again my lot. The Twentieth Century – as you liked to call it – was entertaining, but the killing and nationalistic stupidity tended to make me want to change the channel. Speaking of channel changing, your twentieth century media explosion was one of the sorriest moments on the planet.

I must admit that there was some beautiful music that got thrown into the mix. I don't need to name any names, but music was one domain where you people surprised me the most. And I did get a kick out of parts of the recent technological revolution and the great glorious dream of liberty and justice for all. There were amusing moments, especially watching some of the world's presidents giving speeches – with straight faces no less – about "freedom" and "democracy" all the while knowing that the poor little sheep glued to their smartphones were no more free than shell-on walnuts. As always "freedom" had meant free to do what the hell somebody's laws and traditions said you could do, but nobody bothered to think about that.

Overall, I saw a lot of repetition, a lot of crawling around looking for food, a lot of obedience to flags and gods, and a hell of a lot of waste.

So, the convention starts tomorrow... You can imagine why I'm looking forward to seeing what happens. I do like where they're having it: the mountains, the valleys, the lakes, the rivers, the photogenic castles, the vineyards that survived the flood, the geraniums, the flower clocks in the parks, the lazy grazing fields for cows and horses, the yellow-bright colza in spring, the waterfalls, the parks, the cheeses, the chocolate.

It was surprising how many people in this area had survived the flood given the shenanigans of Zwingli and then Calvin a few centuries ago. But a surprising number of the Swiss came out alive and didn't end up floating too far from their homes.

In case you're not familiar with the area, I hereby put on my narrator's hat. Lake Geneva (formerly Lac Leman and a bit bigger now) is about seventy miles long and sits under the morning shadows of the French and Swiss Alps. A string of towns, each one cuter than the next, had been propitiously built along its picturesque shores. Each had had a church in the centre, a few cobblestone streets, a lakefront promenade, a park or two with flowers galore, and plenty of benches for strollers to park their bodies on and enjoy an ice cream and the astounding views. The flood got rid of about half of this, but the area today is still "very nice".

Geneva is at the south end of the lake. The conference is to be held twenty miles to the north in what had been a basketball gymnasium for the local team in the town of Nyon. The hall had perfectly withstood the flood thanks to the brilliant architectural work of its designer, Monsieur Jacques Suard, a former basketball player himself. There are bleachers on the west side that seat about twelve hundred people and on the soft wooden floor, where the players used to scuttle and scurry about in their cute little shorts and tank tops, chairs have been placed to accommodate the rumps of another thousand or so. This should do it as the guest list has been announced to have two thousand and eighty-five names on it. A little boy, Chipper Lattner, accounts for the uneven number. Everybody else is coming in twos. A podium has been set up on the east side of the gym at the spot that used to be the scorer's table for the old sporting events.

I'm only indulging you with this to give you a perspective and a notion of the environment for the meeting and maybe, at the same time, to whet your appetite, as mine is already, for what is going to take place. Who knows, something "historic" might happen. At least we'll see where the world might be headed.

21

The evening before the opening of the conference a banquet was held in a huge tent that had been set up by a local company, Baltisberger, in a parking lot between the Nyon train station and the gym. By seven o'clock all the delegates had arrived and were mingling between the tables and at the spacious entrance, with glasses in their hands full of a delicious local white wine, a Sarraux-Dessous from the village of Luins. "Flutes" – crisp salted breadsticks – and peanuts were lounging in bowls at numerous strategic locations waiting to be nibbled and slow the effect of the wine on the brains of the excited guests. The party was intended to be festive, but many of the participants came from areas where very little wine was consumed and, as is well known in Europe, the Swiss wine is so "drinkable" that downing a half a litre before dinner is as easy as counting one-two-three.

Farley and Tammy, with Chipper navigating between his mum's legs, found themselves in the middle of the crowd and were conversing with an oriental couple whose English was choppy to say the least.

"What part of the globe do you come from?" Farley asked looking down at the coal-black hair of his interlocutor.

"What globe?" the man said.

"Well, the only one represented here, I guess." The man looked more confused. "What 'globe' mean? I no know word 'globe'."

"Oh, my fault. Globe means world. What part of the world are you from?" A big smile creased the man's face. "Oh world...yes...yes...world...I come from China part...nice part of world China part...China still have people...many people...but not people oceans like before." He looked at Farley with blinking eyes, continued smiling, and asked, "And you...you and nice woman...what globe part you come from?"

"We're from the east coast of America."

"Oh yes...that good...America...I thought maybe America all dead people now...oh, that good...good America here." A waiter came by and refilled their glasses with wine. The man gulped a couple of gulps and then laughed. "This wine like water...ha-ha-ha..." His head rocked like it was on a string. "We have no this kind of wine in China...this make man want make baby...ha-ha-ha..." The woman next to him smacked him in the chops. "Ha-ha-ha...that my wife...ha-ha-ha... Woman not like man...ha-ha-ha... Woman like make baby without man... ha-ha-ha... immacule cassepsun... ha-ha-ha... world still same... ha-ha-ha..."

"I'll give you one thing, it is awfully good wine. What were your names? I don't think I got your names," Farley said thinking maybe it might not be a bad idea to divert the conversation.

"Me Chou Foo. This Lili Lee."

"Lili... I had a girlfriend in grammar school named Lili... beautiful name. Well it's a pleasure to meet you both. I'm Larry Farley and this is Tammy Lattner. Hope we'll be seeing you around."

Farley and Tammy delicately ambled towards a bowl of breadsticks putting a few feet between them and their Chinese friends. "This might be fun," Tammy said, delicately crunching a "flute" between her teeth.

"Might be? It already is. Talk about getting a chance to see..."

Before he could finish his sentence Chou Foo was back next to his elbow bent on introducing him to somebody else. "Larry, want you meet Pappa Dapp Omuk from Eskimo."

"From where?"

"Eskimo. Pappa Dapp Eskimo. We meet yesterday in hotel. Pappa Dapp say it too hot here. Hotter than witchy tit...ha-ha-ha..."

Farley put out his hand and shook heartily with the "Eskimo". "Where would that make you from, Pappa?"

"Pappa Dapp!" Chou Foo interrupted. "Yesterday I do same mistake and say 'Pappa' and Pappa put me straight line and say 'No Pappa, Pappa Dapp!'"

"Sorry. Pappa Dapp. I've got a feeling that names are going to be tough around here. So where did you come here from?"

"I coming from Greenland," he said proudly in an English that Farley could see after six syllables had Chou Foo's beat by a breadstick.

"Well nice to meet you. Tammy, say hello to Pappa Dapp from Greenland."

"Nice to meet you sir."

"No 'sir', Pappa Dapp..." he smiled a smile that had teeth everywhere. "Your boy child?" he said looking down at Chipper whose head was pressed into his mother's thigh.

"Yes. That's my boy Chipper. We decided to bring him along."

"You Larry married? He look older for you," Pappa Dapp said with a wink of the left eye.

"No, no. We're not married. We're just here together from our cluster."

"Cluster. What cluster mean?"

"From our group. From our area, just like you're from your part of Greenland, we're from our part of America."

The glasses were filled again. The service was royal.

"Well, nice to meet you," Tammy said to Pappa Dapp afraid to make a mistake if she used his name.

"You too. You husband dead?"

"Yes, he is."

"So my wife."

"Sorry."

"No be sorry! No be sorry! You sorry?"

"Well, not really."

"No be sorry, no be sorry," he repeated. Tammy was saved further attack as the public announcer tapped the microphone a few times and then asked everyone to be seated as dinner was about to be served.

The dinner was salad, veal in mustard sauce, rice, spinach and, for dessert, cherries soaked in kirsch. With dinner the wine turned red, a pinot noir, also from the Sarraux-Dessous domain. By the time the speeches came round with the dessert, most everybody seemed in high spirits and merrily intoxicated. The first speaker was a local woman who thanked everyone for making the journey from their homes, wished a warm welcome, and said she hoped the meal had been enjoyed. The crowd clapped madly and some people tapped their glasses with their dessert spoons. The second speaker was a man from the northern outreaches of Europe – Norway or Finland perhaps – who tried to get the crowd into a more serious mood and talked about the great responsibility that they all had in reshaping the world. He said that the flood should not be seen as a tragedy, but rather as a chance to turn the globe around (when he said "globe", Farley, sitting across and three people down from Chou Foo, gave the Chinese man a solid thumb's up sign) and to create a kind of heaven on earth. He went on for about five minutes. When he finished his audience let loose another rousing applause. The last speaker was an organisational guy who told everybody that if they had any sleeping or transportation problems they should come to the front table immediately at the close of his speech. He then reminded everyone to be at the gymnasium at nine o'clock the next morning where they would be given their name tags and the conference would officially begin. "We have work to do," he said. And he wished everyone a good night.

At least it can be said that for three and a half hours all corners of the world had been stitched together with the long hearty thread of good food and well-chosen wine.

Tomorrow would be another day.

22

The people attending the conference were not the type to believe in omens, but they couldn't help but notice what a beautiful day it was. The lake was as calm as a dead butterfly and Mont Blanc, Europe's highest peak, could be seen fifty miles across the way.

"See that?" Tammy said to Farley while they waited for their shuttle bus. They were lodged in Arzier, a village a few kilometres above Nyon with only one hotel, a rustic chalet-style building appropriately labelled "Bel Horizon" because of its large terrace and open eastward view.

"Hard to miss," Farley said. "Haven't seen many things to match it. That big white glob is Mont Blanc, isn't it?"

"Good a guess as any. It's the tallest mountain in Europe according to my guidebook."

"You've got a guidebook?"

"No. But I read a little before coming over. How'd you sleep, anyway?"

"Like a baby in a bag of marshmallows. What about you? Did Chipper wake up during the night?"

"Once, about four. But I was awake anyway. We found our way to the bathroom. What time is it? The bus should be here."

"Eight-fifteen. We're all right. We're only ten minutes away."

A very varied crew had shared their assigned hotel with them. There were twelve rooms in the hotel and when Farley had wandered down the hall to the toilet before going to bed, he had heard a half dozen different languages bouncing off the walls behind the doors of the other rooms. People seemed to still be in a festive wine-fuelled mood and were in no hurry to go to sleep. He and Tammy shared the same room which had two single beds pushed together to make a big double. Neither of them had made an effort to pull the beds apart, but each respected the other's space like cars in a parking lot. Chipper had a child's mattress on the floor next to his mother. There was a small table and a chair by the window, an old, tilted armoire opposite the beds, and in the corner a basin with a quaintly faded mirror above it. Shower and toilet were out the door and down the hall to the right.

The bus pulled into the hotel parking lot at eight-thirty, quickly inhaled the twenty-five passengers, and wound down the hill to the Nyon basketball gym, home of the first new world convention.

Things were organised. Everybody registered at tents outside, got their name tags and found seats in the gym. Chipper sat between his mother and Larry down on the floor at about the free throw line on the north side.

There was a lot of chatter. People waited. Farley and Tammy saw none of their acquaintances, except Pappa Dapp the Greenlander whom they caught a glimpse of as he was walking down the bleacher stairs smiling but looking overdressed. "It'll be interesting to see who's running this show," Farley whispered. Tammy nodded her head and kept looking at the spectacle of the stream of multifarious guests. At about nine-fifteen, the Scandinavian man from the night before, tall, blondish, slightly beer-bellied, slowly walked to the podium and the crowd leisurely fell into silence. He waited, checked his notes, placed a hand at each side of the lectern, then finally bent over to where his mouth met the microphone:

"Ladies and gentlemen from around the globe (Farley's thumb, lazing in his lap, automatically shot two inches skyward), welcome to the first conference to form a new world. And when I say new world, I say it with a capital "N" and a capital "W". We have before us perhaps the

greatest challenge that the human race has ever known. Human beings have built pyramids and skyscrapers; human beings have painted the great works in the Louvre, the Prado, and other museums; human beings have written literary masterpieces; human beings have gone to the moon and have set the world wide web in motion; human beings have colonised and conquered; but...but...ladies and gentlemen, human beings have never created a world of harmony, peace, love, and total respect for life on this earth. (Applause fills the hall, slowly at first because in these early days some people still had trouble understanding English.)

"We all now know that the great flood of three years ago left only a certain kind of human being on the earth. It has been calculated that eighty-five per cent of the population was killed. And who was killed? Two types of people: people who believed in mythical gods and people who coveted other people's possessions. This was deduced – I should say 'induced' – by a man, one Larry Farley, on the American continent a few months after the flood. (Tammy reached across Chipper's thighs and dropped four fingers on Farley's hand.) All of us here have then two things in common: we don't believe in gods and a special life after our deaths and we are honest with the affairs and possessions of other people. We have an incredible opportunity, a marvellous chance to build a NEW WORLD... (Applause.)

"So how are we going to do it? Who is going to lead us? What kind of leaders do we need? Do we need leaders at all? What common bonds will bind us together? What will our priorities be? What laws must we enact to bring about our goals? What are our goals? Can we do what the old United Nations was unable to do? Can we create a world with no war and no poverty wherein each world citizen can live a productive and happy life? But what does 'productive' mean? What, in fact, does 'happy' mean?

"Ladies and gentlemen, we have two weeks to address ourselves to these and other great questions. We cannot fail in our quest to set the foundations for the future. We cannot let down our fellow citizens back at the homes whence each of us came. (This guy must be one of those Europeans who ended up with an MBA from Harvard, Farley thinks.)

"I have been asked to officiate only for this first day of our conference. At the end of this day we will elect a chair to officiate for the remaining fortnight.

"For the present, I want to ask everybody to take five minutes and think about what you want to have on the agenda for this first meeting today. We did not want to make an agenda without the conference's approval. Remember, we will be in session until noon. We will eat in the tent around the corner. We will begin again at two this afternoon. And we will finish at six o'clock tonight. Does anybody have any objections? No objections, then five minutes of recess for you to think about today's agenda."

Seems like a nice guy, Farley thought.

I wonder what I'm going to do with Chipper all day, Tammy thought. I've got to find a babysitter.

"So what about the agenda," he half shouted to her as the hall started filling with chatter again.

"We need a name. What do we call ourselves?"

"Good idea."

"Then we need rules."

"Yeah."

"Then we need to decide what's important."

"I can't wait."

Chipper needed to go to the bathroom. Tammy led him around the floor to the corner of the gym to the little boys' room where in days of yore, the big boys, the basketball players, used to drop their loads before games. It is well known that pre-game jitters worked wonders on the bowels.

Tammy and Chipper retook their seats just as the Scandinavian man brought the group back to attention. During the five-minute break he had turned on an overhead projector and a woman at his right had opened a laptop and seemed to be ready to act as his secretary.

"Thank you, ladies and gentlemen. Let us come to order. (Order came quickly this time.) Our immediate task is to fix an agenda for the day. Who would like to make the first suggestion? (There were eight people with purple T-shirts on, each holding a microphone, ready to run and hand it to whomever the Scandinavian man gave the floor to.) Yes you, the woman to my right...oh, please identify yourself before you speak... (How can you identify yourself before you speak? Farley thought. But he knew what the guy meant. Farley hadn't noticed that it was Tammy who had put her hand up and who was about to stand up and grab the microphone.)"

"I'm Tammy Lattner from the east coast of America. I think the first thing we need to do is give this conference an official name. After that, I suggest we make some simple procedural rules as to how we go about things."

"Thank you, Tammy. Does everyone agree? No objections? Okay, what do we call ourselves? Yes sir, in the back to my left."

"I suggest that we..."

"Could you give us your name sir?"

"Oh yes, excuse me. I'm Kimoto Nakamara from central Japan. I think we call us 'The World Visionary Council'."

The secretary typed *The World Visionary Council* onto the displayed slide.

"Yes, you sir."

"Mein name ist Friedrich Heinrichbacher. I say we..."

"Where are you from, sir?"

"Oh yes, I ist from north Germany Hamburg."

"Thank you, sir."

"I zink we call our name 'Za Great World Conference for Brozerhood, Peace, and Love'." (Somebody had obviously helped him with the name which he did a great job pronouncing.) The secretary hit return twice and typed *The Great World Conference for Brotherhood, Peace, and Love.*

"Any other suggestions? Yes, you madam, in the front here." A microphone flew into her face.

"Hi, I'm Helen Hoffer from west Canada and I think we should call this convention 'The Mother Earth Survivors' Convention'."

"Thank you, Helen."

Among other suggestions were: The United World Conference, The First True World Peace Conference, The Last Chance Lucky Survivors Rodeo (this came from an Argentinian who still seemed sauced from the night before, but who acted dead serious when he had the microphone in his hands), The United Planet Convention, The Planet United Convention, The Convention for a

United Planet, The Useless Dot in the Middle of the Universe Conference (this came from a guy who was obviously stoned but was beautifully dressed in a Hawaiian shirt and white shorts)...

...And on and on went the suggestions until somebody from Ireland pointed out that it was *already ten-fifteen and we have a lot to do.* Amazingly the vote went rather quickly because everybody seemed so tired of thinking about a name that almost half the audience went with Kimoto Nakamara's initial suggestion, "The World Visionary Council".

So "The World Visionary Council" it was and the vote was followed by a ten-minute break.

"You just stood right up with no fear of anything," Farley said to Tammy as they rose to stretch their legs.

"I was secretary of my high school student body. When you've talked to one group, you've talked to them all. My mother used to give me the old speech about imagining that the whole audience was on the toilet, I mean that we're all nothing but humans. It always worked for me."

"Good for you."

"Thanks Daddy," Tammy said and gave Farley a quick kiss on the side of his unshaven face. Then she gave Chipper a bottle of water that she had in her purse. "I've got to find him a babysitter. He'll go crazy in here before we do."

"Don't be so sure. Actually, I think this is going to be fun. Anybody need the toilet? That coffee we had this morning needs a new home." And off Farley wandered to the little boys' room.

By noon they had fixed a few rules and the agenda for the rest of the day:

RULES:

1. All votes require a simple majority of the members present
2. In case of a tie, vote again (somebody will change their mind)
3. Interventions from the floor should be brief - three minutes maximum
4. All voting shall be open with raised hands
5. The council will have a break every 90 minutes

AGENDA FOR THE DAY:

1. world identification cards
2. helping people learn English
3. world – or local – traffic laws?
4. equal health opportunity around the globe

5. world – or local – schools? what are the schools going to teach?
6. how to avoid the errors of the past – what were the errors of the past?
7. vote for chair – and co-chair – to lead the rest of the convention

There was definitely a spirit of good will roaming through the hall and when the Scandinavian adjourned the meeting for the two-hour lunch break, everybody clapped, and certain areas of the world cheered and stamped their feet, much like fans of yore, in the same hall, used to manifest their pleasure and excitement when a local player did a high-flying slam dunk or hit a game-winning three-point shot as the last second ticked off the scoreboard clock.

23

I think I need to clear something up before we go any further. It has to do with some of you harbouring a perception of me as a hard, uncaring, immoral, unfeeling, insensitive killer of billions of people. How, you ask, could I have done away with so much of the human population and still be able to look at myself in a mirror and live with the monster staring back at me?

I will explain. I beg you to listen.

Let me put things comparatively, allegorically, or in terms that might make some sense, after reflection, to your way of thinking.

Let's imagine there was a world somewhere, floating through a very large universe, a nice big round planet inhabited by a rather vast amalgam of creatures. Some of the creatures grew out of the ground, some flew in the air above the ground, some lived in the ground, some lived in a liquid form of ground much like our water, some walked on the ground, some were many times bigger than others, some were many times smaller, some made sounds that were shared by others, some made no sounds at all, some had small teeth, some had big pointed teeth, some had poison in their salivary glands, some ate the creatures that grew out of the ground, some ate the creatures that lived in the ground, some ate the creatures that flew, some ate those that lived on the ground, some ate the creatures that crawled or swam about in the liquid ground, some lived very short lives (days, minutes, even seconds), some lived longer lives (years, decades, even centuries in the case of some of the things that grew out of the ground), but all eventually died away and were replaced by other similar breathing creatures.

Well, all of this mixture was tied to a planet, floating through the large universe, living and dying, eating and being eaten, flying and crawling, swimming and walking, talking and not talking, and...and...suddenly some creature has a bright idea. She, he, or it...it makes little difference to our story...decides that some of the creatures of the world have more value than others. Up until this creature had his (its, her) bright idea, nobody had talked about one group having more value than another. All living things had simply been trying to survive as best they could, in their own way, with the bodies and minds that they found themselves with. But this creature who had the bright idea suddenly decided that all other creatures that were not like it (her, him) were of less value than she (he, it) was. Then, he (it, she) decided that these other creatures should be placed in a hierarchy of value. That is, the little ones were of the least value – they could be killed by the millions and nobody gave a flying rubber duck fuck – and the bigger ones (there were usually fewer of the bigger ones) were of more value, but never of the same value as the one who had had the bright idea or the rest of her (his, its) kind. And then, as a finishing touch, he (it, she) decided that on top of the totem pole there was a god and this god gave his blessing to the whole hierarchical jumble.

So, to make a long story short, the creatures of the same type as the thing (gal, guy) that had the bright idea all started to share this bright idea. It made them feel good because they were near the top, just under God, of the cute little value-ladder and they could henceforth kill and eat any of the creatures underneath them and essentially never really feel badly about doing so. The little creatures that were bothersome could be stepped on or sprayed or doused or poisoned and none of the bright-idea creatures batted even the slightest eye. The mid-size and over-size creatures that were found to be pleasurable eating for the bright-idea creatures found themselves slaughtered by the millions and billions and again, no one gave it a second thought because the bright-idea gal (guy, thing) had convinced them all that the mid-size and over-size creatures had, in fact, essentially been created for their dining pleasure.

So, if you get the crux of my story, you might think for two minutes and see that if the bright-idea people can do away with millions and billions of creatures without batting a pretty blue or brown eye, then I, too, can do the same. I, too, can decide what is of value and what isn't. It just so happened that I decided that certain types of bright-idea people were of less value than others. And so I created a nice little flood to send them on their way – just as they had done to other creatures in their own time – to a swift annihilation.

And so just like a person who works in a slaughterhouse or sprays bugs from an airplane or beheads chickens on a poultry farm does so without the slightest pang of conscience, so I too sent a few billion to their end. Like the "bright-idea being" in our imaginary world floating through our imaginary universe, I set up a system of values and then acted and made decisions in accordance therewith.

That's all I have to say about that. For now, anyway.

24

It turned out that the Scandinavian chairman-for-the-day wasn't really Scandinavian at all. He lived right there in Nyon and had been the son of a former United Nations diplomat who had been born in Stockholm and had moved with his Göteborgian wife to Switzerland in the 1960s. The son had never even had a Swedish passport. The native tongue had, however, been spoken in the home and, having gone through the Swiss school system, he had ended up fluent in four languages: Swedish, French, German, and English.

Farley caught up with him toward the end of the lunch break to see if he had any ideas for a babysitter for Chipper. "My daughter," he answered immediately. "She's fourteen and we live right up the street. She just finished a year's 'stage' in a bakery and right now she's doing nothing. I'll talk to her tonight and your boy should have a place to hang out starting tomorrow morning."

"He's not my son, but thanks."

"Whose boy is he?"

"The woman I'm here with. The one who made the first suggestion this morning about finding a name for the conference and making a few rules."

"Oh, yes. An attractive woman. You're lucky."

"Aren't we all?"

"In a way, I guess."

"Well, thanks. I'm sure Tammy will be happy."

"Who's Tammy? I thought the kid was a boy."

"He is. Tammy's the attractive mother."

"I'll bring my daughter with me in the morning and she can take the boy back home with her. We really only live a couple hundred metres away."

"Many thanks. I'm sorry, but I never got your name."

"Henrik Hansson. And you?"

"Larry Farley."

"Larry Farley? You're the Larry Farley that put two and two together and figured out what the flood had been all about?" Farley nodded coyly. "Well I'll be damned. Nice to have you with the group."

"I kind of got roped into it, but now that I'm here I'm having a wonderful time."

"So where are you from. I don't remember exactly."

"The eastern part of America now. But I was born and lived a long time out on the west coast."

"Nice area. I was a big fan of San Francisco."

"A lot of Europeans were. They thought it was sophisticated."

"Wasn't it?"

"Depends on what you mean by sophistication."

"I guess so." He looked at his watch. "Listen, I'd better get moving. We'll have time to talk I'm sure. You can count on my daughter in the morning."

"Thanks," Farley said. And he watched Henrik Hansson trot out of the eating tent and turn left towards the gym.

The afternoon session of the World Visionary Council started with a discussion on world identity cards. It was curious how not one of the two thousand plus present was in favour of bringing back "countries". It was as if the survivors of the flood were all so happy to be alive that they couldn't imagine setting any kind of boundaries between themselves and any other survivor. Their good fortune had been equal – life – and they wanted to keep it that way as much as possible. It took under a quarter of an hour to decide that everybody in the world would have a card with a name, a date and area of birth, and a recent picture. But everybody would be free to live and work and play wherever the hell they wanted to and were able to.

Point two: helping people learn English. This was also a piece of cake, except for a French delegate with an accent as thick as a slab of Chateaubriand who immediately got up and rather diplomatically questioned the choice of English as the world language. He was immediately hooted and booed into submission, especially by the Inuits, Siberians, and basically everybody from cold weather climates. Why English was so popular in the land of snow and ice is anybody's guess, but the Frenchman took the derision good-naturedly, and actually laughed and took a bow, and when he fell back into his chair, shouted, "Vous gagnez!" He was warmly applauded.

A delegate from Holland suggested that television and films were the key to getting English into everybody's head. He explained that where he came from kids often watched cartoons and adults usually watched films in their original language – which was usually English. He explained that viewers were more likely to listen to what Mickey Mouse, Daffy Duck, Brad Pitt, or Marilyn Monroe were saying than to some teacher standing in front of a bored classroom. He suggested that teaching be done first through this kind of immersion method and later with grammar and spelling lessons. The crowd clapped enthusiastically and no motions were made and no vote was taken.

The third point on the agenda, typed in bold by the secretary on a new slide, was traffic laws. How the hell could we get people to stop killing each other with cars? Do we slow everybody down to a maximum of eighty kilometres an hour? Do we work to get people to simply enjoy being where they are (even if it's in a car), instead of watching people fall back into the pre-flood mentality where everybody was always in a hurry to get somewhere else? Do we make people take driving tests every five years? Do we ban alcohol? (This question, especially after last night's wine, brought loud boos from all sectors of the gym. You'd have thought that the star player on the local basketball team had just been thrown out of the game for giving back an elbow to a guy that had previously given him a series of flagrant unprovoked blows to the chest and abdomen.) Do we put padding around all vehicles such that if they ever do collide it's not going to be metal and glass against metal and glass, but rather rubber and sponge against rubber and sponge? Of course this would be costly, but surely within ten short years all cars could have some sort of mushy carcass. Do we put radar devices in every vehicle to warn people of any approaching danger? This, given that a lot of technology such as driverless cars had been washed away in the flood, might take too much time before it became effective. Should cars be removed from the face of the earth? (Boos from everybody except the hemispherical extremes.)

It was decided that speeds would be greatly reduced because this crop of humans wasn't so bent on being in five places at once, that cars would be padded with neoprene or some such substance that would make any eventual collision more like a "bumper car" experience at the old county fair, that people could not drive until they were nineteen years of age, that the same driving course and test would be given everywhere and the driving licence would – like the personal identity card – be universal, that drunk or stoned drivers who were responsible for any problem on the road would be immediately put on garbage collecting duty for one year, that nobody could have more than one car, and that trains and public transportation would be a major priority all over the world and that they should be as cheap as practically possible.

The conference ploughed into equal health opportunities around the globe. It turned out that, in theory, this was essentially a no-brainer: everybody corroborated the idea that every man, woman, and child should have the same access to the same quality of healthcare. Of course, putting this into practice was another story, but at least all ships were pointed in the same direction. A man with a beige cowboy hat on who introduced himself as "Big Bobby Britches from the Middle-of-Fuckin'-Nowhere-Nevada" said that where he came from, before the flood, a lot of cows got better healthcare than some of the people, and he "ain't sure it weren't a good thing" given that "half the two-legged sonsabitches he used to see in the streets was a helluva lot more useless than a goddammed good cow". He was roundly applauded and raised his beat-up Stetson to acknowledge his listeners. Henrik Hansson saw Farley put up his hand and gave him the floor. He said that as far as he knew it was nowhere written into the fabric of the universe that people should be valued over animals. He said that the nature of things – that is, humans having more "power" than animals – didn't necessarily mean that they were worth more than animals unless power was considered synonymous with worth. Then he said he didn't have a solution to the problem, but that keeping an open mind about the whole ethical bag of potatoes was probably a good thing for a civilisation. The cowboy then proposed a vote that cows be given equal medical treatment to "all us sonsabitches". Given the ambiance in the hall, the motion passed by a landslide. A New Zealander immediately proposed that sheep be accorded the same deal. He, however, was greeted with a string of "Baaa-Baaaa-Baaaaa" sounds from different zones in the bleachers, and his motion was hastily defeated.

Healthcare would be equal for people and cows. Farley was surprised nobody brought up cats and dogs, but they didn't. So on the afternoon meeting moved to the problem of schools.

It quickly became obvious that this was a bigger morsel to chew... Do we go back to the kind of schools we had before? But schools in Finland were a far cry from schools in Tijuana, Mexico. Or Harlem. Or Washington D.C. Or Kolkata. So who had had the best schools? And why? What should be taught? What should be learned? When should the learning be learned? Did it make any sense to teach world wars to ten-year-olds? Teaching Flaubert to fifteen-year-olds probably, more than anything, resulted in the kids never picking up a Flaubert book again. We certainly can't teach history like we did before with good guys and bad guys painted with bright provincial colours. And what about history that forgets 99.99999% of the people who have lived on the planet? And the animals? (Animal ontological stock was definitely rising.) What place do animals have in history books? Up until the flood all they got was a page or two of pictures of extinct dinosaurs. If we go back to schools for kids, we have to stop wasting so much of everybody's time.... 95% of everything pre-flood teachers said – particularly to students aged from 7 to 17 – didn't even get in one ear and, hence, didn't have a chance to go out the other, and was never applied to any moment in the student's life. Do we need schools simply to babysit kids? Do we want mothers back in the homes? Do we want to admit that a parent at home might be one of the most important things that a kid can have? Couldn't parents spend more time teaching their young kids given that young kids like security? Could the working parent pick up the slack at night? Is it feasible to have two parent homes? At what age should children choose a profession? Should people learn more than one profession to make life more interesting? What does the word "education" mean anyway?...

The remarks were vast and varied and the discussion started to warm the auditorium. A Greenlander (Farley presumed it was Pappa Dapp's partner because they were sitting next to each other) said that school was the worst thing that ever happened to his kids. He said they were pleasant, happy, obedient children until they began going to school at age eight. Then they started mutating into useless brats. He didn't mince his words and the audience gave him a thunderous cheer when he said "mutating into useless brats". (Farley wondered where he picked up his advanced vocabulary, compared to Pappa Dapp's, that is). A very old woman from Turkey with a beautiful turquoise shawl around her shoulders and an operatic deliberate voice said that whatever they decided about education, they'd better be careful, take their time, and make decisions only after serious reflection.

It was decided that the subject would be put on hold until the second week so that the conferees could have time for ample contemplation.

More than two hours had passed. Tardily and mercifully, Henrik Hansson declared that it was time for the afternoon break. He gave the crew thirty minutes.

When they came back into session things went much more smoothly and there was much less discussion. The subject about not repeating "errors of the past" took a lot less time than could have been expected. This was largely due to the fact that people were starting to get hungry and some were licking their lips thinking about the evening's wine selection. The errors, it was decided, were far too many to count, were made on essentially every square metre of the globe at almost every moment in human history, were, in a sense, paid for by the flood, and would not be repeated. Other than believing in bogus gods and coveting other people's stuff, nobody seemed much in the mood to start to enumerate past civilisations' stupidities. It was commonly intuited that that was why there were all assembled in the first place.

At five-forty-five, Henrik Hansson announced the last point on their first day agenda: selecting a chair and co-chair for the remainder of the conference. The cowboy from Nevada made quick work of this: he stood up and said, "I don't know what alla you all think, but I thinks weze awready got the right man right here in fronta us with Mista Hank Hansson." Cheers, foot stomps, hands clapping.

Henrik, without a vote, had secured the job.

25

Farley found a payphone tucked under the stairs that wound down from the entrance lobby to the locker rooms where the ballplayers used to change. It worked with quarters. He called Billy B's knowing that it was six hours earlier on the east coast and at noon, their time, he figured he had a good chance of catching his buddies in the restaurant.

"Billy B's Bar and Grill. Eat your heart out til your heart wants to eat you," Billy B said on answering.

"Billy, it's Larry. Sounds like you're right next door. Just wanted to see how things were going."

"Son of a bitch. We all thought the Titanic sank. So you ain't dead. It's about time you called."

"Well, you know how it goes when you're travelling. You forget how long you've been gone."

"Screw you."

"Unfortunately it's not happening. So who's in the store? I figured it was a good time to call."

"Well, let me gaze across the horizon. On a bar stool in front of me you have the world's favourite, most underworked cop, better known as Bill the policeman. Olga, the planet's finest waitress, is getting ready for the lunch rush by filling the napkin holders and the salt and pepper shakers. Our dear friend and fry master, Philip Papp, is scraping the grill with one hand and beating his petrified meat with the other. Who do you want to talk to first?"

"You, of course. So what's new? How's the weather? How's business? Has Olga got a boyfriend? Any crime in the streets? Anything new on the menu?"

"Larry, there's as much action here as there is in Santa's workshop the day after Christmas. What about you? You savin' the world?"

"If you want to know the truth, this place is a riot. It's like going around the world in a baby stroller."

"What the hell does that mean?"

"It's a kick, a barrel of laughs. The place is full of characters."

"How's your partner, Little Miss Tammy?"

"She doesn't snore, her feet don't stink, she doesn't leave her underpants on the floor, she rinses the basin, and we use the same toothbrush."

"You dirty son of a bitch."

"Not yet, unfortunately."

"You guys in a hotel?"

"The 'Bel Horizon', baby. We've got a view of half of Europe and Mrs. Blanc."

"Who's Mrs. Blanc?"

"The French woman that undresses in the window across the alley every night while I'm saying my prayers."

"Listen, Bill wants to talk to you. He's been drooling on the floor since I picked up the phone. Here he is."

"Larry Farley, our representative in heaven, how's the world looking?"

"We'll save all you sinners from yourselves before we finish. We're making rules to bring about the most wonderful world outer space has ever seen."

"I thought we were inner space."

"Inner, outer, what difference does it make?"

"So what kind of rules are you making?"

"Well, this afternoon we decided that any policeman caught looking at a waitress's rear end has to clean toilets for a week."

"When do I start?"

"How is Olga, anyway?"

"She's still the only reason I get up in the morning. Yesterday she came to work wearing leopard shorts."

"Leopard shorts? How'd she look?"

"I don't know. I only saw the shorts."

"How'd they look?"

"Straight out of the jungle."

"When will you men ever change?"

"Why would we want to?"

"So you'd get your mind off the leopard and go build a railroad or something."

"That's why we build railroads. To go find new leopards."

"She must be sitting on your lap."

"Here she is. She wants to say hello to her favourite ex-client..."

"Olga? Are you there?"

"Hi honey."

"Hi Olga. I hope you're taking care of the inmates."

"Hi Larry. We miss you. No one to talk garbage with."

"Thanks. I miss you too. How do you like the work?"

"Has plus and minus. Plus is I sleep at night. Minus is people like you don't give me hundred bucks for ten minutes' work."

"You said it wasn't work..."

"I lied. But sometime more work than other."

"Hey, when I was going to college I used to work in a hamburger stand and I loved it. Just watching people's mouths open wide and their eyes slightly closing and seeing their jaws slowly clamp together on that first bite...it was such a pleasure to watch the eating pleasure. You know what I mean?"

"Larry, I give enough pleasure for all the hamburgers in China before I start serving hamburgers..."

"Gotchya. Listen, is Philip around? I'd like to just say hello."

"Okay. When you come home?"

"We're trying to make the whole earth everybody's home, but we'll be here a couple more weeks."

"Well, hurry. The ice cream melting...here's Philip..."

"Hello, Larry Farley. Are you president of the world yet?"

"Not yet. How do you like the grill? What I used to like was wiping the half inch of grease off my forehead after the lunch rush."

"One of life's pleasures."

"Has Olga been good for business?"

"Has wine been good to man? Of course she has. Nobody cares what the food tastes like. They're too busy looking at her leopard shorts."

"Bill told me."

"You and Tammy having fun?"

"Honestly, it's like the Epcot Center with real people. It's a kick. Well, look, I've got to get to dinner. Say goodbye to everybody. By the way, how's your son and that girlfriend of his?"

"Not much news."

"No news is good news. Oh, I almost forgot. Tammy wanted to know how Betty Swain is."

"Let me ask Bill. Bill, have you seen Betty Swain around?"

"Yeah. Saw her yesterday. She looks great."

"He saw her yesterday. She looks great. Good. All right, Philip. I godda go."

"See you, Larry."

"My heart's on that grill."

26

It was love at first sight, kind of.

Nadia Hansson stood with her father in front of the gymnasium waiting for Farley, Tammy and Chipper. She was a fourteen-year-old who not only had not yet sold her soul to a boy but swam outside the current of teenage tyranny in things both musical and vestmental. She was nobody's slave, a bit like a five-year-old who never grew up. She was about five foot two, wore the most ordinary blue jeans and yellow blouse, had her brown hair pulled off her face in a ponytail, and flashed a cover girl smile across her innocent face when she saw the three coming her way; Chipper flanked by the two adults, his hands held on each side.

"Good morning you people from America. This is my daughter Nadia." The teenager extended her hand to Chipper first.

"This is Chipper. I'm Tammy, Nadia, and this is Larry Farley. Thank you so much for coming. I surely hope it's no bother to your summer plans."

"No, not at all. I just finished a baking course and I'm free until I decide what to do next." The girl's English was impeccable.

"So I guess today's kind of a trial day to see how you both get along. Is that okay? Then if everything goes well, we'll work out the details of how we can compensate you when we meet this evening. How about six? Is six okay? We'll be finishing at six, won't we Mr. Hansson?" He nodded. Tammy handed Nadia a bag and explained it contained a sweater, Chipper's favourite game, a book, and his little nameless but irreplaceable teddy bear.

They'd meet in the same spot at six. Tammy kissed her son. Nadia took his hand and, like newlyweds on a Balinese beach, they shuffled off into the belly of a bright aestival morning.

"That was easy," Farley said as he slid into his chair at the northside free throw line.

"She seems adorable. I can't believe her English," Tammy said now sitting next to him in her son's place.

"It's those Scandinavians."

"I thought you said he was born here."

"He was."

"So he's not Scandinavian."

"Actually I'm Scandinavian, too. On my mother's side. Her parents were Norwegian." He was whispering now because Henrik Hansson was at the podium ready to call the congregation to order for day two of the World Visionary Council.

"You're so full of crap," she whispered back, he feeling the air from her mouth trickle past the hirsute strands growing like baby cattails, at attention like Vatican guards, valiantly protecting the entrance to his left ear. For the first time Farley felt a flicker of affection from his partner in the quest for world...*world what?* he wondered as he briefly shivered at the idea of her warm breath brushing his skin. Then he thought again: So what were they really trying to accomplish for the world? Peace? Most probably. Safety? Yes, but safety was never going to be guaranteed. Food for all? This was likely to come up on today's agenda. Healthcare? Of course. Shelter for all? Yes. Transportation rules? Yes. Brotherhood and freedom of movement for all? Maybe a little tricky, but yes. But after that? What? Were they out to snuff ignorance, idiocy, illiteracy? The physical stuff would probably be reasonably easy. But the mental stuff? The mind? The morals? The meta...physical? But nobody in the crowd believed in God. Did that mean there would be no talk of the "metaphysical"? But metaphysical doesn't necessarily have to involve gods and otherworldliness. It can involve simply thinking about what anything and everything and nothing is. If it's not God's world, it's still a fucking world. Everybody in here probably has a different idea of exactly what this godless world is. Taking God away doesn't solve anything. It's just a beginning. A "now what?" Okay, there's no God or gods, but what is there? This too is metaphysics. Will the World Visionary Council address this mess? Only time will tell, thought Farley, the old philosophy professor in him not totally extinguished. And then he rethought the thought of Tammy's whisper and the lips that had done the gossamery deed.

"Ladies and Gentlemen," Henrik Hansson began, "it's an honour to stand before you again today. I thank you for your trust and confidence in nominating me chairman for the duration of the World Visionary Council. As we did yesterday, we will immediately establish the agenda for today's meeting. I'm sure you've all had time to formulate your ideas. Our schedule is the same as yesterday, nine to noon, lunch break, and two to six. Who has the first suggestion for the agenda for the day?"

"Yes, to my left in the rear."

"It's not exactly about the agenda, but I was just wondering," said a man's voice, the microphone not reaching his lips until the word "wondering". "I was just wondering if we were ever going to get up into those beautiful mountains together, as a group, I mean. Every morning when I wake up and see those Alps I say to myself, 'I've got to get up there and hike around', because where I come from it's flat."

"Where do you come from? And please, by the way, please remember to introduce yourself before speaking." (Farley's mind again twitched at the beauty of Henrik Hansson's admonition to introduce oneself before speaking.)

"Oh yeah, sorry. I'm Bill Bertlestein from the midwest part of the USA. I just wondered if we might do a tour together or when we might have some free time to get up there."

"I appreciate your appreciation of the scenic beauty of our area. My intention was to work together for five days then have a one-day break and then go for another five days." Groans floated like low clouds through the auditorium.

"Yes, you sir here in the front."

"I Vladan Durcic from Macedonia and I propose we work four day, then we have two day free for visiting." A roar of approval rang like a liberty bell. (Farley was amazed how awake everybody was.)

"I assume we won't need a vote on that one," Henrik said diplomatically. "So, if there are no objections, we will work today, then two more days, then you will be free for two, then we will go four more. No objections? Fine. So back to the agenda... Yes madam, in the middle with the turquoise shawl."

"I'm Anika Polikar from Turkey."

"Yes, you spoke yesterday."

"Yes. I think we should talk about the abolition of the word 'race' from all human discourse. The word is a vestige of human stupidity and I think it should be put in the garbage once and for all. We're all a mixture; there is only one race, the human race. It's a detail, but I think it needs addressing."

"Thank you, Anika. (We're starting to get first-name cosy, Farley thought.) Any objections?"

Silence. ABOLITION OF WORD RACE appeared on the overhead screen.

"Yes sir, in front on my right."

A tall thin man rose from his chair laboriously, "I'm Manute Sol from the Sudanese part of Africa and I think we need talk about the problem of my continent. Not just my area, but my continent. In my time of life I see most of the world get many things for many people like lot of food and hospitals and nice houses and long lifes. In Africa, I see progress very slow compared with rest of the world. The flood help equalise things. This is sure. We in Africa start to make better place to live. The flood take away the poisonous people who steal and kill. This very good. I ask we find a way that more engineers, doctors, builders, and such necessary people come to Africa and help us help ourselves..." He choked up as he said this last sentence and the crowd applauded warmly. He stood there rocking gently on his spindly legs and wiped his eyes with his sleeve.

"Thank you," Henrik said. Any objections to Mr. Sol's suggestion to discuss Africa's needs? Fine."

AFRICA HELP was added at point two.

There was a thirty-second silence before anybody – Henrik included – said anything. Finally a woman in the back stood up.

"I'm Tatiana Kruschki from Russia near St. Petersburg. Before the flood, life was very difficult for most women from my country. We were often physically abused and given no more respect than toilet tissues. Of course, the flood helped us a lot. All the brutes were drowned. But I worry about it starting up again when the young generation now grow up. How do we avoid falling into same pattern? How can we keep the bad away? Thank you." She sat down quickly. When people realised she was finished, scattered applause became general applause.

"I think this problem fits in with the general problem of education that we talked about yesterday. How can we prevent the upcoming generation from becoming problematic human beings? If it's okay with you Tatiana (was it only the females who got the first name treatment?), I suggest we put your suggestion as part of the education discussion." Henrik saw Tatiana nod in approval. She seemed happy to have said what she said to the big crowd.

The following other subjects became the rest of the day's menu: LABOUR LAWS, LIMITING SCREENTIME, THE ROLE OF THE MEDIA, and FREEDOM OF SPEECH. It was nine-thirty. They were ready to roll into day two...

...And when they rolled out of it, at five-fifty-five that evening, the following conclusions had been reached:

1) The word "race" would no longer be used to define a human being. Nobody knew how long men and women had been around, but however long was long enough to have mixed up the genetic soup beyond recognition.

2) Africa would get special attention. Though humans were free to go where they wanted, a major effort would be made to get the necessary trained people to migrate there as quickly as possible. It was pointed out by a Swiss garage mechanic, of all people – who said he had spent all his vacation time over the last decade on the continent, primarily in the Cameroon area – that African women

knew what men wanted, etc. Amazingly, this was not greeted by a chorus of soprano and contralto boos, but rather with a silent forest of coy smiles on the majority of the male faces. The women chuckled politely.

3) No one would be asked to work more than eight hours a day at anything, even though it was universally agreed that work was necessary for human health. Children, from age nine on, would work at least two hours a day. It was thought that this would give a sense of collective responsibility, but at the same time would leave them plenty of time for play, which they would appreciate more than they would if they didn't work. At age fourteen they would work three hours a day. At eighteen they would work six. At twenty they would be considered adults. Any schooling at whatever age would not surpass four hours a day, this being an arbitrary, but reasonable, limit for juvenile concentration. The problem of money and wages would be brought up later.

4) Television and social media had to be controlled. By whom? How? To what end? This was a sticky topic. Was the pre-flood mess a media problem or a human head problem? Were they the same problem? Was broadcasting only a reflection of who people were? Did programmes make people or did people make programmes? Couldn't

what we watched be used to promote the general good? What was the general good? (Farley had smiled waggishly at this whiff of ethical query.) Should programmes only be streamable after dark? Should television be limited to three channels? Five? Ten? Two dozen? Had television, more than anything else in the pre-flood world, contributed to the making of a brain-dead civilisation? Had civilisation ever not been brain dead? Was humanity simply simple and had television simply been proof? Would not the people left on the earth produce different and "better" media?

All these questions took over an hour and it was decided that given the complexity of the issue, a commission would be formed at week's end to tackle the problem in depth.

5) The press was easier. It would be as free as the wind. The written word did not have the same deleterious potential as visual media. The written word, with music and painting, was historically at the heart of all worthwhile civilisation. Sure there was a lot of shit. But its smell travelled much more slowly than that of the televisual shit.

6) Speech would also be as free as air. But, it was pointed out at ten minutes before six, wasn't television part of free speech? Obviously it was linked. We'll let the commission think about it. Time for dinner...

27

"I think we found the right Chippersitter."

"I think so too."

"He was beat. They must have played for hours."

"Let me help you pay for her."

"Not on your life. He's not your doing."

Unfortunately not, was the first thought that piped through his head. "But your coming here is," he said.

"I could have stayed home."

"But you didn't. Let me help. Nine hours a day is a lot."

"She didn't even want any money. We finally agreed on twenty dollars a day. I can handle it."

"Not if I have anything to say."

"You don't. You won't. But what you can do," she said sipping her wine and staring out at the lights of Thonon and Evian on the other side of the lake, "is take me on a walk up in those mountains. I'm glad we've got the two days off. We can make a weekend of it." Her sweater was dangling over her shoulders and she pulled the sleeves closer to her chin.

"Are you cold? Would you like to go inside?" They were on the restaurant terrace of their hotel. The day had been gorgeous. The night followed suit, but they were two thousand feet up and it was almost ten o'clock. Chipper slept above and behind them in their second-floor room.

"No, I'm fine. A view like this on a night like this shouldn't be wasted."

I hope I heard that right, he thought like a kid overhearing Santa Claus say he was getting a new bike for Christmas. "All right, it's a deal. My treat for the weekend in the mountains. Hotel, meals, and ski lifts included." Tammy didn't say anything. She raised her head and sniffed the moon. Then she laughed.

"A guy told me you can ski on the glaciers in the summer. At least at the Matterhorn."

She swallowed wine and ran her tongue along her upper lip. A Japanese couple rose from the table next to theirs, looked their way, bowed, and said goodnight. Half the terrace was still occupied.

"Do you ski?"

"Not since college."

"Where was that?"

"University of Utah."

"What were you doing out there?"

"My boyfriend was on a football scholarship."

"I hope he wasn't a defensive tackle."

"He was the quarterback, cutie pants."

"So what happened?"

"We broke up after our sophomore year. He fell in love with himself."

"That's the beginning of a long romance. That's what Oscar Wilde said anyway."

"Actually he wasn't a bad guy. But I didn't want to spend my life with him or his future. I think I was smart enough to realise that the odds of a college romance succeeding was about like getting four aces on the first deal. It's amazing how dumb we were."

"Were?"

"Were. Are. You know what I mean. But I didn't do much better when I finally did get married. I was twenty-eight, tired of running around, wanted to settle down – all that kind of thing. I kind of took the first train that came through the station not knowing where it was going."

"Chipper's father, you mean?"

"You're almost as smart as I thought you were. Yeah, Chipper's father. Wrong train. Took us out into the desert of 'Nothing-To-Talk-About-After-Two-Weeks-Of-Marriage'. But, hey, I got Chipper and his father went with the flood. Things didn't work out so badly."

"Maybe we should put marriage on the agenda tomorrow."

"Maybe we should put love on the agenda."

"And blindness."

"And mental retardation."

Their laughs crossed in mid-air. Farley got the waiter's attention and ordered three more decilitres of wine. He knew enough not to expect anything even though he knew he wanted something. He also knew that he had been as cool as a popsicle to have not made the slightest advance in all the time they had known each other. He also knew that when she had whispered in his ear that morning his body had jangled like the change in a hot dog vendor's pocket.

"Do you think the flood has done anything?"

"There are fewer assholes around to get mixed up with." The way she said the word "asshole" made it sound like the "ss"s were "zz"s and it was a noun worth waiting for.

"Are there? Sometimes I wonder. Actually I don't. But I do wonder where the world will go. We're still on the honeymoon."

"So it was really you who first figured out that the flood nailed all the believers and coveters?" Farley was surprised this was the first time she mentioned the subject since Henrik Hansson's declaration the day before.

"I guess so. That's what people say anyway. I just started looking around at the survivors – talking around I should say – and I realised nobody was aggressive and nobody was trying to peddle an afterlife. It wasn't that hard really."

"So who did it? The flood, I mean."

"If I knew that I'd be King of the Prom. But it's worth wondering about. Somebody or something sure as hell took good aim and knew which the hell pieces were going to get washed off that chessboard."

"Have you thought about it?"

"Of course I have. It gives me the willies. What do you think?"

"I figure that who or whatever did it can't be all bad."

"Well, at least we know that maybe even if there's not a reason, there's at least a rhyme."

Tammy stared at her wine glass as the waiter filled it. "What does that mean?" she finally said.

"You know, like, You want more than this life? Here comes the knife."

"You're terrible."

"Or maybe, Wanna steal Jack's cave? Then take this wave."

"Larry..."

"Hey, until the flood hit I didn't believe in anything. The only directions the universe had were signs to the toilet and the cemetery. Then, after the deluge hit, I thought, 'God damn, maybe there's a shepherd leading all these blind sheep after all'."

"So all your philosophy studies had led you nowhere."

"Nowhere is not the word. I was at the bottom of the fucking bottomless pit. The deeper I dug, the bigger the hole got. Finally the hole was so big all I could do was stare at it in paralysed amazement. Honestly, before the flood, I had absolutely no idea what to think or believe about anything. I was in dreamland, honey." The "honey" slipped out like a bedwetter's pee, but landed rather nicely on the cool evening air.

"Well, me too, really. Of course I didn't believe in God. Love had been scratched out of the dictionary. Friendship was looking a little shaky. I had Chipper, that was about it. Fortunately it was kind of enough."

Farley loved the "kind of". He wanted to kiss it with his wine-sweetened lips. Instead he said, "My kids were already away and I'd been divorced for quite a while. What saved me was that I'm kind of like you and your sky."

"My what?"

"Your sky. The first time we met in the park – way back when – you said you loved the sky."

"I did?"

"You don't remember?"

"Not at all."

"I thought that's what you told everybody. I thought it

was your standard tell-everybody-who-I-am line."

"Hardly. I can't even remember saying it to you. Are you sure it was me? I'll bet you have had lots of deep conversations with all those cute mothers watching their kids on those park benches."

"Honey, I even remember you saying you loved every sky – green, grey, blue, black, or panty pink."

"Panty pink?"

"I had an art history teacher in college whom I remember nothing about except one day when he stood in front of the class and started his lecture by saying, 'Take a pair of red panties, take a pair of yellow panties, take a pair of blue panties, take a pair of pink panties'. I have no idea what the point was, but I never forgot the pink panties. It just popped out."

"Was he a lush?"

"Not at all. To the contrary. He was this real conservative-looking mid-western suit-and-tie guy. And as dry as a wishbone."

"Well, if I really said I loved the sky, I must have been inspired."

"Let's hope so."

"You think you inspired me, don't you? You egotistical, megalomaniacal, so-cock-sure-of-yourself-fiftysomething-year-old-ex-professor you."

"Worse things could have happened."

They stayed on the terrace for another twenty minutes. Time ticked away like a baby's heartbeat. Was love made that night? There had been no choice. Did they wake up Chipper on his mattress on the floor? They didn't think so.

28

So, in a sense, I've been found out. There are those who
know that there are causes unseen. But so what? It's no big
deal. Nobody knows where I live or what I look like or
what kind of deodorant I use. And they sure as hell won't
find out. They talk about their black holes and anti-matter
and all that kind of thing, but they'll never have a
microscope or a telescope powerful enough to peek at the
likes of me. Actually, lately I've been thinking that maybe
I should show my face. Boredom is swelling my feet. How
would you feel if you had watched the circus for a few
billion trillion zillion billion trillion zillion years? You
people don't even have a number for the time I've put in.
Your clocks don't go past midnight. Your whole calendar
isn't even a note in the symphony. But it's not your fault.
You were hatched that way, with bad eyes, bad ears, and
short fingers.

I must say, though maybe I shouldn't, that when I watched the man Farley and the woman Tammy tinker around last night, I was almost jealous. But not in a covetous way. I mean they reminded me of what I had hoped man and woman would be capable of doing to each other but had no control over. They got a glimpse of the other side. They made me wonder if it wasn't all worthwhile.

29

The following morning they awoke just in time to catch the bus down to Nyon. Chipper had climbed into bed with his mother. She had stirred and looked at the clock. 8:32. "Whoa, hurry up, Chipper. Get dressed." She and Farley bolted the bed and trotted down the hall to the toilet in their underwear feeling their sore parts. They threw on their clothes and rushed to the bus, the door sliding shut like a vault as soon as Farley, nose to Tammy's behind, had mounted the first step. The other passengers gave a hearty applause.

Nadia was waiting for them in front of the gymnasium as bright and beaming as a headlight. Chipper ran to her and shouted, "Nadie!"

"We overslept. We almost missed the bus," Tammy said. "Chipper hasn't eaten anything, so he might need a little cereal or something."

"No problem. We have plenty of things, Mrs. Lattner." Nadia said taking the boy's outstretched hand.

"We'll see you at six tonight then. Bye Chipper."

He didn't need to say goodbye. He and Nadia ran through the parking lot and up the street.

"Do you think the kid's in love?" Farley asked rubbing an eye.

"He might be. The lawd works in strange ways."

"Doesn't he now! I had thought I was as erotically dead as a Thanksgiving turkey. And now look at me. Ready to yawn and snore through today's session after last night's marathon."

"Marathon? The first time was more like a forty-yard dash. I think you broke the world record."

"I told you, I was out of practice. Thanks for giving me a second chance." He winked, but she didn't see it.

"You did better, darling."

She grabbed his arm and they went inside the hall with the last stragglers. "The world's at stake in here, don't forget," she said.

"I had forgotten. My ego was blinding me. You plucked out my eyes, you wicked wench from the north. Where'd you say you were from?"

"Idaho."

"That's far enough north."

She gave him a peck on the cheek. As they started down the bleacher stairs he obsequiously pinched her butt; she fly-swatted his crotch. They walked to their seats as if nothing had happened, nothing except the sun's rounded head climbing up behind the Alps a couple of hours before giving the earth another chance at another diamond day.

"Before we make the agenda, I have a special request from one of our members. He has asked me if he can talk to the congregation for a few minutes before we put our noses to today's work. This is the first such request and I see no reason to refuse it. If there are no objections I will give the microphone to our representative from the area of Greenland, Mr. Pappa Dapp Omuk." Pappa Dapp waddles to the podium like an over-fed penguin.

"Goo morning, goo morning, my brother and sister. (Tammy squeezes Farley's hand.) I stan here to tey you what come up from the boddum of my heart. (He smiles wide and his eyes pinch shut.) We, we the Woood Vishionary Council, work togedder for two day only. Two day. What two day in hitory of life? Nutting. Nutting at all. But no. These two day are probabby greatest two day man ever do. I think we can finally give world a chance to be world of peace and love and love and peace where Eskeemo and African and red person and yellow person and white person (Farley wonders where the pink-panty person is) can join hand and live tugedda in hamony and responsibitty and democracy and libaty and mastabation for all. Thank you, thank you."

As the applause becomes a crescendo, Farley whispers to Tammy, "Is he campaigning for you or the presidency of the world?"

"Both, I hope," she whispers back.

"Best speech I've ever heard in my life," he blows past his cupped hand. They both clap sporadically with the rest until silence returns.

"Thank you Mr. Omuk," Henrik Hansson's voice fills the auditorium, a mouse's roar in a tame jungle. "I'm sure everyone in this room agrees with you and that we share the same goal of world peace and universal love. Now it is time to establish the agenda for the day."

Farley daydreams through the morning session. First he sees an image of a passage from somewhere in Nietzsche's writing wherein he says what an unliveable world it would be if everybody really and truly did love each other. You wouldn't be able to walk down a street without being hugged and kissed by everybody...it would take hours...days even...to walk to the grocery store and back.

Then he wonders about world peace. Since the flood there has been a sort of tranquility that has not as yet translated into an omnipresent boredom. This is likely because there has been so much work to do to get the planet functioning again. But now that things are functioning, will ennui start to show its pale face? He looks round the hall. How long will these people be content to live without conflict? When will some of them (him?) get their kicks out of messing with their fellows? There have been tribes in the Amazon that seemingly lived for centuries without war. Were there chiefs who crushed the first sign of disturbance with an iron fist? Or had there really been no disturbances? Sects end up imploding for one reason or another. Is power, when all is said and done, not at the root of everything? (Nietzsche again.) Since the flood, maybe it is, in fact, power that the survivors have been feeling as they sense their utility in rebuilding the planet. But now that the planet is coming around, will their energies move on to different quests, quests that entail overpowering others? Even they, possibly, have been trying to overpower the flood as they have laboured to erase all trace of it. Animals are still being eaten. Hamburgers are still being served. Fish are still being pulled out of the sea. This is beautifully rationalised and justified. When will killing other humans get the same treatment...?

...But what an interesting time. To get to see the world in a pristine state. Whatever force was behind the flood, did it intend for war never to come back? Or was it just clearing the chessboard before the start of a new game?

How long in the past have there been moments of real "world" peace? How soon now before conquerors arise in their midst? Maybe if Pappa Dapp gets a taste of Tammy's delights, he and I might try to kick each other's butts to get a monopoly on the goodies. I haven't seen sex turn to fighting since the flood. Will this group share each other's women? (Men?) Or will the absence of coveters keep all those heretofore exploratory pricks in their owners' pants?

He turns his head and looks at Tammy's lips, then face. Yes, a possessive gurgle bounces around in his gut. He wants her again. For the first time in who knows how long he has the urge to "have" a woman. Of course he had wanted Olga, but he knew that she, by her own choosing, was common property and that he had never had any intention of messing with the formula....

...Maybe, before, excluding the three years since the flood, people essentially misjudged what they were really made of. Maybe Christianity, with its notions of God creating us in His own image, had planted the absurd idea that human beings were something special, that, as "God's children", we had it in ourselves not to be warlike, when in fact if "man" was anything he was a warrior in that he always wanted his own stuff and more. Maybe civilisation has never defined us as what we really are. Maybe we have always attributed to ourselves qualities that we attributed to our phony gods. Maybe we are nothing but worms on the sidewalk – trying to get from here to there with nothing much more on our minds than survival...

Larry Farley thinks of his children and his late wife. Why, he doesn't know. His wife Carole's face flashes before him as he sits with arms folded staring at the back of the head in front of him. She was a warrior, fighting every second to beat to death her jealous fires that were no more her doing than lightning bolts were. They separated, like most couples, because somebody was hurting too much somewhere. Nobody asks for their own pain. Nobody draws it up in a laboratory. It's just there, working its slithery havoc all the way to the courthouse....

...And Ricky and Rosanne. His children. We love our children more than anything else because we know they are innocent. We know they didn't ask to be born or to be born who they are. Man and woman make love and the darting sperm fight for property rights on the patient little egg, waiting coyly like the last strawberry in a bowl, until one of them blasts through and plants its nation's flag that says You're mine now, baby. So life does begin with war: gladiator sperms going at it until there is only one survivor. Why should the rest be any different?

Before the ten-thirty break, Farley has fallen asleep on Tammy's shoulder. She arouses him as the others are rising and filing toward the exits.

30

Jay Papp and Violetta Poole leave the motel and walk across the street for breakfast. The Pancake House is blue and yellow inside and most of the tables are occupied. Commerce is crawling back. The "Please Wait to Be Seated" sign stares at them as they stare into the room without seeing. The hostess arrives and leads them to a corner booth and says "How's this honey?" to no honey in particular. Jay says "That's fine" and the hostess moves away. She is quickly replaced by a waitress who plops down two glasses of ice water and two plastic-coated menus. "I'll be right back with you for your orders," she says thinking about table twelve behind her and walks away with a slight limp.

Jay and Violetta look at their menus, but neither is thinking food. Jay peeks at Violetta's face over the top of his menu that he is holding in the air with two hands. Her unmade-up face is beautiful. Her hair and a hand are hiding half of it, her menu open flat on the table. Jay feels he is losing her. She is like a boat that has been untied at dock and has started bobbing and floating out to sea. Last night she only wanted to make love once and it seemed her fervour had cooled. Jay Papp had pouted and Violetta Poole had thought him childish. Their weekend at the beach is not what Jay had been expecting.

"What are you having?" Jay says trying not to sound like he is floundering at the short end of the lollipop.

"Pancakes."

"Whadaya want to drink?"

"Orange juice."

The waitress is there again with her pencil aimed at a little pad of paper that is cupped in her hand up near her chin. "Are you ready to order?" she says for the eight-thousandth, nine-hundred-and-fifty-fifth time.

"Two orders of pancakes, an orange juice, and a cup of coffee please."

"You want the short stacks or the regular stacks?"

"What's the difference?"

"The short stack you get two and the regular stack you get three. They're big."

"Regular stacks will be fine."

"I'll take a short stack," Violetta says.

"One short, one regular," the waitress says as she scribbles on her pad. "I'll be right back with your drinks." She swipes the menus with a paw like that of a cat swatting a dangling ball.

The menus have been a buffer, but they aren't there anymore. When Jay sees Violetta's eyes look past him, he feels weak. When he looks at her he loves that body so much that he takes a deep breath and when he exhales people at the next table can hear it.

31

A good half of the World Visionary Council have left for the weekend, most to the mountains. Henrik Hansson organised a few buses and hotels for those who wanted to be together. They are in Zermatt to glimpse the Matterhorn. Farley, Tammy, Chipper and Nadia have taken a train to Sierre and are sitting on the right side of a yellow postal bus that takes up more than half the road in many spots as it winds its way to a village called St. Luc. Farley had asked a few questions of some locals and St. Luc came up more than once as a quaint picturesque village with a view of, admittedly the back side of, the famous mountain, without the crowds.

It is eleven o'clock Saturday morning. The sky is cloudless. The bus wheezes and grinds and sometimes seems ready to lie on its side and float to the depths of a two-thousand-foot canyon. But it doesn't. It stays on the road, honking as it approaches the blind corners where it fills the entire street. What few cars there are wait before the turn until the mammoth has set itself straight and has passed.

"If nothing else, it's worth the ride," Tammy says. "But I don't think I'd do it again." She is next to the window and has stopped looking down.

"I've seen mountains, but these are mountains," Farley says. Chipper and Nadia are in the seat behind them tickling each other. They turn left at the village of Vissoie. The sign says seven more kilometres. The chalets all have red geraniums just like they're supposed to. "Seven more kilometres...holy shit," Farley mumbles.

"What got anybody up here in the first place? This town must be more than a hundred years old," Tammy says.

"I just saw a sign on a chalet that said 1887."

"They walked up here?"

"Donkeys, horses maybe."

"They must have wanted some privacy."

"Or grass."

"They wouldn't have to come this far for grass. How do you know?"

"I don't."

"Whenever you see a picture of the Swiss mountains you always see cows and grass. Maybe you have to go above the forest to get good grass. And we're not above the forest yet."

"And to make that Swiss cheese those cows need grass."

"Seems like there'd be enough grass down in the valley where we came from."

"Seriously, do you think the people came up for themselves or the cows?"

"Probably both."

"Maybe they just wanted to look around and they liked it. Maybe they brought the cows along so they wouldn't have to go back down to get a drink of milk and a slice of cheese."

"You're a genius."

"I'm an idiot."

"We're both idiots."

"Where'd you say you went to college?"

"I don't remember."

Out of Vissoie the bus came to a complete stop for a turn that looked impossible to negotiate. The driver backed up, went forward a few feet, backed up, then made the turn.

"You'd think they'd get smaller buses," Tammy said.

"It wouldn't be as exciting."

"It's not like we had to reserve a seat to get on. There are eight people on this bus, plus the driver."

"Maybe there are more in winter."

They pulled into the village and the driver let them out in front of the Hotel Bella Tolla. "I say we get a room in the Hotel Bella Tolla," Farley said. "It's cute and it might be the only one."

They went inside and the lobby looked like it must have looked a hundred years ago. "I'm in love," Tammy said as they approached the check-in desk. Chipper and Nadia jumped into two big red armchairs straddling a carved wooden table with magazines on it.

"Glad to hear somebody in this world is," Farley responded.

"Not with what you think," she uttered tenderly.

"I knew it wasn't with me. How could anyone fall in love with me?" He rang the bell on the counter that said "Sonnez".

"I thought you loved me. I thought you thought I was the most gorgeous woman ever to ride that bus up to this heavenly hideaway."

"I do love you. More than a dog loves food. If you'd have let me, I would have humped you last night until death did us part..."

Farley didn't know if he had finished talking, but a smiling elderly lady came from a back room to the front desk and said, "Bonjour tout le monde."

"Sorry, but we don't speak French," he said.

"No problème," she said. "I learn English in school sixty-years ago."

"We wondered if you had a room for the four of us, with a view if possible. Just for tonight."

"Every room have a view and I have room for you. You want to see it?"

"No. We trust you."

"You have euros or dollars?"

"Both."

"One hundred euros for four of you with breakfast included. Okay?"

We're on the top of the world, Farley thought. The sky's the limit. He hadn't worked on the exchange rate. "Perfect," he said pinching Tammy's cute little buttocks hiding like a walnut behind her tan jeans.

They were ushered up one flight of stairs and given an old, long key with the number 14 on it. "Good room with bath," the woman said.

What's the key for? Farley thought. "Good room with bath," he said.

"Breakfast from seven to ten. Check-out noon."

"Fine."

The woman walked across the room and pulled the curtain. She opened the window and poked her head out. "That mountain with the point in the back is the

Matterhorn. Americans always want to see the Matterhorn. It called Cervin here."

"Really? Why is that?" Tammy asked.

"Why are you calling chips French fries?"

"You got me."

The woman saw Tammy looking around the room that had a double bed and a single near the window. "I bring you a portable bed for your little boy. Okay?"

"That'll be fine."

"This our biggest room. Plenty of space."

"Plenty of space," Farley echoed and the woman disappeared.

"Do you think the weather's always like this?" Tammy said lifting the handle on the door to the balcony.

"How could it be?" They both stepped outside. "Look at all the snow on those mountains. And it's the middle of summer."

"It must be eighty-five degrees."

"Never thought it'd be possible up here."

"So what do you want to do?"

"Look at the mountains and you naked," he said looking at the mountains.

"When will you grow up?"

"That's just the problem. I am grown up. I know what counts."

"You're sixteen."

"Without the pimples. Look, we've only got about twenty-four hours up here. I say we go explore." They walked back into room 14.

"Kids, let's go," Tammy said.

"Already?" Chipper chirped. "We just got here. I'm hungry."

"We'll find you something."

"Let's go climb some mountains," Farley said ushering the kids out into the hallway. "Tammy, I'd bring sweaters along just in case."

"Yes dear."

"Maybe we should have got two rooms," Farley said as the kids plunged down the stairs, Tammy stepped out, and he didn't lock the door.

"Don't be so presumptuous. What happened yesterday and the day before won't necessarily happen tonight."

"That's why I love you. The mystery is eternal."

They left the hotel and headed up the narrow street through the village. There were fountains and geraniums everywhere. Some of the chalets were squat and quaint. Others were on stilts.

"Nice town, isn't it? I think we made the right choice," Tammy said.

Near the end of the village there was a little grocery store. A woman had just stepped out and was starting to lock the door when Tammy ran up to her. "Could we quickly get something?" she asked. The woman looked at her and the kids and Farley and nodded her head. "Maybe a sandwich? Do you have sandwiches?"

She opened the door and led them in. The store couldn't have been bigger than two cars parked next to each other. On the right there was a glass case with some ham and cheese. Behind that a few loaves of bread were stacked on a rack. "Some bread and cheese would be fine," Tammy said. The woman nodded and went behind the glass case and pulled out a round slab of cheese setting it on a cutting board. She grabbed a heavy knife and spread her thumb and forefinger to suggest a thickness to cut. "That's fine," Tammy said. The woman dug the knife through the cheese and wrapped it in a piece of shiny white paper, Scotch taping the ends. Then she grabbed a loaf of bread behind her and slid around to the cash register.

Farley had wandered to a shelf with wine and selected a bottle that unscrewed on top and said "DOLE" on it. He grabbed a packet of cookies and a big carton of iced tea. "This should do it," he said.

"Merci," the woman said. She rang everything up and pointed to the number on the register. "Vingt-quatre quarante." She smiled and put the items in a plastic bag.

"Sounds fair to me," Farley said dropping some bills into the woman's hand.

"Merci," the woman said. "Bonne visite."

They stood outside the little store and looked up at the mountains. "I say we climb that one," Farley suggested pointing upwards to his right at a round peak that had some kind of a building on top.

"Can I have a cookie?" Chipper said.

"Me too," Tammy said.

"Nadia?"

"Yes please."

Farley tore open the cookies and deposited two in each of three open outstretched hands, then popped one into his mouth for good measure. The quartet ambled down the little street past a chalet that said "Agora" on it, munching and skipping and bright-eyed, much like princes heading towards a healthy harem.

32

It was at that precise moment that Betty Swain died: 6:09 on the East Coast; 12:09 Swiss time. She made the slick transition from sleep to death with no more than a shudder and a quick pinch of the eyelids. She didn't even get her hands up to her heart. Had she not died, she would have awakened at her usual time of a little before seven. She would have rolled to her right and looked at the clock and seen that the day had finally come. But she didn't. She died instead.

She was not found until six days later, this corresponding with the end of the first World Visionary Council. When Farley called his friends back home that Saturday evening, word of Betty's death had made it into Billy B's greasy spoon. Of course Tammy, who was standing next to Farley for the phone call, was the only person who knew what Betty's last wish was, to wit, two songs sung by a group of children holding hands around her coffin. She took the phone and told Bill the policeman that this was what she wanted. Bill said he was sure they could keep her body on ice until Tammy got there, even if it was in two more weeks.

Two more weeks would come two weeks later and Betty's desire would be rightfully honoured.

But we're not there yet. For now we watch the motley quartet make its way up to the summit of the Weisshorn, eight thousand feet above the level of the supple swollen sea.

33

For what are mountains if they are not women? What are women if they are not mountains? What more could either ask to be?

And men? He couldn't think of anything.

It took two hours to get to where they wanted to go. The hike had not been hard in that they were always on a well-trodden path that zig-zagged through the forest and, when the forest was below them, gracefully brought them to the top of the Weisshorn without any steep climbing. But they were hungry and thirsty and it was almost two-thirty in the afternoon.

The building that Farley had seen from the village was an abandoned hotel that had been in use before the flood. In winter, skiers were brought up in snowmobiles every evening before dark. In summer you had to hike up as there were no roads. But the Hotel Weisshorn had done well for many years because of its amazing view and the reputation the food had of being "hearty and tasty in the alpine spirit". Likely the hotel would one day open again when winter sports returned to the world scene. But for now its doors were locked and there was nary a soul inside.

"I'll make some sandwiches," Tammy said spreading her unused sweater on the grass that was sprinkled everywhere with edelweiss.

"I'm thirsty Mommy."

"Larry, can you open the ice tea?"

"I already opened it halfway up the mountain."

"That's right."

"Come on over here Chipper and drink to your heart's content. It's good we got a big carton. Nadia, there's plenty left."

"Thank you Mr. Larry." The kids drank, then ran off to play behind the hotel.

"Don't go too far!" Tammy yelled. Then to Farley, "I like that. I'm going to start calling you Mister Larry."

"And you? Do you go by Miss or Mrs. or Ms. Tammy?"

"I'll go with Miss. Makes me feel younger."

"All right Miss Tammy, how about passing one of those delicious butterless bread and cheese sandwiches over here?" Farley unscrewed the cap on the wine bottle and took a swig. He felt like King Arthur. "Do you want some Miss Tammy?"

"Yeah, just let me finish here."

Farley drank some more and finally fixed his eyes on the view. There was not a sound; he knew not the name of anything he saw; he saw for miles and miles; nothing moved; sky, mountains, snow, forests, village; blue, grey, brown, white, green; blue, grey, brown, white, green; thick as soup; but when he threw his arms out in front of him, he felt nothing; but he knew it was thick as soup.

"Here. Here's your sandwich, Mr. Larry."

"Thanks. Look at this. Just look at this. Here, here's some wine."

"Thanks."

"Nothing's moving."

"I thought everything was always moving."

"That's just it."

"Here, have some more wine."

"It's excellent, fruity. Must be local. Dole." He drank, then he looked. "It feels like it could suck us all up."

"It could. It will."

The kids shouted behind the hotel. Farley looked at Tammy. Tammy looked at Farley.

These things don't happen very often.

34

The World Visionary Council had two more days together. They had bitten; they had chewed; they had ruminated. They had voted. Housing, agriculture, food distribution, transportation, health-care, the media, communication, monetary exchange, taxes (everybody would give ten percent of everything they made to the local cluster and the cluster would give ten percent of that to the world council). The only thing that was really left was the human mind. Or, if you will, education. When Henrik Hansson called the group to order at nine o'clock on Thursday morning of the second week, his tone was sterner than it had been. He put his nose to the microphone, turned his head left, right, then back to the centre and said: "Ladies and gentlemen, we've accomplished a lot so far and we have two more days before us. As we said before, we would save the topic of education until the end. Hopefully we have all had enough time to think about which direction or directions we want the world to go. All the adult survivors have two things in common: they don't believe in an afterlife and they don't covet other people's possessions. We have millions of children that need to be educated, that must be educated, that are looking for guidance one way or another. How shall we proceed? What kind of teaching must be provided such that the world does not fall back into the dark ages of false belief, war, thievery, and... and...ignorance? The floor is open."

The audience had picked up on the seriousness of the chairman's demeanour and intentions. There was a long silence. Many chins were stroked in deep, silent thought. Finally the woman from Turkey, Mrs. Polikar, raised her hand, was acknowledged, and spoke:

"Thank you, Mr. Chairman. I think we need to look at the state of education in the pre-flood world before we go any further. What was being taught? What was being learned? Who was doing the teaching? Who was doing the learning? Were teachers and parents the real teachers or had not the media taken over the role of transmitting knowledge and values? I remember sitting in school for days – even months – on end and never thinking about the life and value of another creature. I was so obsessed with my own little world of trying to be somebody, somebody 'cool', or obsessed with memorising meaningless junk for tests, that I never thought about or experienced other human beings or any forms of life in a profound way. I, and I think most children, were without a simple respect for the great mystery of life. And I think this only got worse with the years that preceded the flood."

"Thank you Mrs. Polikar (the first names had disappeared). Would anybody like to add to that? Yes, you, Mr. Bobby Britches from Nevada."

"I'm not drunk today (laughs) and I'm thinkin' about the world. Our world. This piece a candy rolling through space at a few thousand miles an hour that we can't even feel. I was thinkin' 'bout my horses and my cows and my ex-wives and all the whores I used to visit up in Mustang and my dead parents and grandparents and my kids...and I was sayin' to myself that I love 'em all and the reason I love 'em all is because of one person, one person about forty fuckin' years ago who told me one day in school to shut the fuck up. I was a wild kid with no respect for nuttin' – including the teachers – and one day I'm disrupting class like always – I musta been about fourteen – and this teacher suddenly grabs an eraser and throws it past my head at about a hundred miles an hour and screams SHUT THE FUCK UP!!! as loud as he can scream. Then he grabbed me by the collar of my shirt, picked me up and threw me right back down in my chair and started screamin' again. Now you've got to understand that this teacher was normally very calm and funny and nice and all, but all that disappeared that day and he was the meanest sonofabitch in the school. Anyway, to make a long story short, he kept screaming and saying that I didn't respect anything on the whole fucking planet except my own bullshit and that I thought I was so cool but was really the biggest asshole in the school. Then he told me to get the hell out of class and only come back when I realised I wasn't the only fish in the goddam ocean. Well, it worked. He got to me. Mr. Frazer was his name. That's what it took for me to start gettin' educated. Without that happenin' I don't know where I'd be today. Yes, I do. I'd be a dead fucker."

He sat down to scattered applause. Henrik Hansson scanned the group. "Yes, madam, you in the middle."

A small woman of about sixty rose. Standing she wasn't much taller than the man sitting next to her. "I'm Claire Friedrich from right here in the Swiss area. I had the opposite experience of the gentleman who just spoke to us. I had a grandmother who was the key to my education. She was quiet, calm, and never raised her voice. I used to watch her take care of her garden when I would visit her in the summertime. When I got older I started helping her with her vegetables and plants. Little by little she explained the respect she had for all life including things that come out of the ground, including the worms and other creatures in the ground. She taught me more than anyone else I know, more than any teacher and more than my parents. She taught me to love life and respect it in all its forms. Thank you." She sat down quickly, catching the audience by surprise. People clapped warmly as soon as they realised.

"Well," Henrik Hansson said, "we've heard two very different experiences with regard to what constitutes an education. I'm sure there are many more that could come forth. But I think we can at least assume that older people do influence younger people and that we older survivors of the flood have a great responsibility to our youth. In my case I would have to say that my mother was my greatest influence. She taught me by example. She was patient, loving and kind with everybody she dealt with... Yes, Tamilia (first names for certain members...)"

"Obviously, what influences each human being is wide and varied. I think we need to address the question of schools. Are we going to bring them back in a form similar to what we had before the flood? Are we going to leave education to parents and loved ones? If, in fact, we are we going to have children start to do a little work from age nine on – I think it was nine – are we going to educate them through their work? Obviously we need to teach English to everybody and some notion of numbers and calculation, but other than that, history, geography, physics, biology, philosophy, cooking, sewing, literature...are we going to teach everybody? Are we only going to teach those whose parents or carers want them taught? Are we going to teach these things only to the children – or adults – who want to be taught? If we are going to teach all young people, then aren't we going to need to set up universal standards to ensure that everybody gets the same quality of education? And who is going to decide what we teach and how we teach? If I remember my time in school in Idaho, very few teachers taught me anything I remember. I did however, somehow, get a general education that has allowed me to get on in the world. I was going to say something else, but I can't remember..."

"Well, thank you Tammy (now it was 'Tammy'). You've given us food for thought there. I suggest we begin with the council's thoughts on schools. Do we, or do we not, want to bring back schools as they existed in pre-flood days? Yes Tammy..."

"Excuse me, but I remember the other thing I wanted to say. Last weekend, when we had our free time, my fellow councilman Larry Farley and I were sitting on top of a beautiful mountain and eventually we started talking (Farley cringes at the thought of the prelude) about how much of our adult lives were really spent unlearning what we had learned in school, and to a certain extent in the home. What we had learned was not 'true' in any sense of the word. What we had learned was rather a series of things that helped us fit into our culture and civilisation, but really not much more than that. I'm not talking about things like what is the capital of France? Or what is 4 x 6? But about how we perceive ourselves and other people in the world. Our ideas – our learning – had really nothing to do with reality. This has been confirmed to me here at our visionary convention in that the prejudicial ideas I had about people from other cultures had all been very wrong. All of you are not what I expected you to be. My 'education' had painted a very bad picture. What I guess I'm trying to say is that I think whatever we do with schools, we should be sure that young people – and why not old people as well – do as much moving around the globe as possible to open their minds, hearts, and eyes to how things really are."

For whatever reason, Tammy had had everybody's attention and was roundly applauded.

"Thank you Tammy. I think I can more or less say the same for myself. Learning requires a lot of filtering and unlearning. And also when you think that what was taught a hundred years ago was not what was taught fifty years ago which was not what was taught ten years ago, the problem is even more complex."

There was a pause. "Yes, Pappa Dapp from Greenland..."

"Thank you Chairman Hansson. I want say two things. One thing that before flood where I come from kids getting badder and badder. This from TV and movies and being together after they watch TV and movies. They all start act like idiots in TV and movies. Other thing, since flood people don't watch much TV and movies because too much work to do. This keep people and young people better people. I think young people must keep active in work like now so they don't start going back to like before."

Everybody liked Pappa Dapp. He raised his hand more than anybody else.

"Thank you, Pappa Dapp. I think we must remember that before the flood a lot of children were living productive lives – whatever that might mean – and that the flood got rid of a lot of those who were spending their time coveting all the crap that the world was producing. This has changed now. We definitely have a chance to move education in a different direction..."

Farley didn't say anything but he thought. He thought that forever it seemed that people have thought the world – life – has a goal, that it is supposed to be moving "towards" something and that this something is more or less written on some gold tablets of life: this is where we should go, this is why we live. Even after the flood, even with people who absolutely didn't believe in an afterlife or a god, he sensed the survivors still had a built-in teleological idea that there was a "design" to nature. Education for what? Towards what? Peace on earth? A world in which people can live for eighty years without getting their shit stolen? A world in which people can "understand" each other better and not be closed-minded prejudiced assholes? Is this the intended goal? ... What if there is no goal? Is this what the human race has been and still is? The great inventors of goals? The great visionaries whose vision is always a purpose to life? Who has ever said that there very, very likely is absolutely NO purpose to the universe? Who could live with such an idea at the forefront of their mind? Many have probably lived with the idea hidden and squirming in a dark back corner of the mind. But who lives with it at the centre of everything they do?

The next thing Farley heard was Henrik Hansson's soothing voice calling for the morning break.

35

What is it about these Americans? What is it that has made them think, and still makes them think, that they are endowed with something special, something that makes them unafraid to be who they are? Most people are coy and reserved. Most people hesitate and doubt before they make their points of view heard. But not Americans. I've watched them for over a century now – even after the flood – walk into any room in the world and think their opinions hold water. In a sense, they stand taller than other peoples. They dare. They lack self-doubt. They stand up when others sit down.

Of course the French have had this a bit too. And the Germans. And the Italians. And people like Pappa Dapp. But as a group, no one beats the Americans.

It must come from their "founding fathers" and the foundation of their civilisation. The Europeans who crossed the ocean looking for a new and better life felt they were "divinely" inspired, that the land that the ships brought them to was a "chosen" land, the corner of the universe that *God* had set up for them. They believed that *God* was watching over it for *them*. This notion has survived. It has survived for two centuries. It has survived the flood. Americans, more than any other group, think they have something to say and they say it with voices unabashed.

This will likely begin to change. The flood will take the wind out of their sails. As the world unites – and it will unite in many ways – those who, however subtly so, see themselves as special, will begin to realise that they are not.

Other than that, I did enjoy Farley's little rumination before the break. Of course there are – and have been – others who believe and live with the idea that existence has absolutely no goal. Me for example. And many Buddhists and Chinese. Living with the idea, in my case anyway, doesn't change a whole lot. It just makes colours brighter, wine taste better, and a day at the zoo that much more amusing.

36

One morning on the boat back Farley looked at himself closely in the mirror in the light of his cabin bathroom. He reminded himself of food that has been left in a refrigerator or on a balcony too long. He thought of shaving, but didn't. Tammy knocked on his door and said they were going up for breakfast. He would join them as soon as he got dressed.

They had planned to stay in Europe for a week after the convention, but Betty Swain's impending funeral had them catching another boat two days after Henrik Hansson swore in Anika Polikar as the first President of the World Visionary Council and Pappa Dapp Omuk as Vice President. Everybody had gone with Farley's suggestion that a woman should have the top spot because there was a theory that her hormones might be less aggressive than a man's. He also suggested that she should come from somewhere other than America or the traditional European powers. He argued for a fresh start, nominated Anika, and she won hands down. Pappa Dapp nominated himself for Vice President and he got the job after a thunderous applause without the council even voting. Tammy probably would have ended up Minister of Education, but she declined her candidacy on grounds that she had to get home quickly and that from all she had heard Finnish schools had been the best in pre-flood days, so why not put a Finn in there. She got her wish with the election of Hanni Kekkonen, a quiet woman from the Helsinki cluster who didn't start talking until the last day. Henrik Hansson was given the post of Justice Minister even though there presently wasn't much for him to do and he had never been a lawyer. Everybody thought he seemed like a loving fair man, which of course he was, and they needed somebody for the swearing in ceremonies.

One post that actually required careful counting of the votes went to Chou Foo who beat Friedrich Heinrichbacher by just twenty votes for Minister of Transportation. Many members of the council had seen Chou Foo soused on a number of occasions, but he finally won on the basis of his training as an engineer. Heinrichbacher had owned a brewery.

The only North American who ended up in the first world government was Bill Bertlestein from Iowa who became Minister of Food and Agriculture. He explained how he'd been a cattleman but had actually started loving his cows more than his neighbours and had eventually gone into corn because he couldn't stand the thought of one more of his animals heading for the slaughterhouse. Nobody ran against him.

When Farley went up to breakfast in the ship's vast dining room, he was feeling a little giddy. He didn't know if it was too much wine the night before or the after effect of looking at himself in the mirror. He held the rail on the stairs more than he normally would have. Maybe he just needed a bit of food in him.

"How'd you sleep?" Tammy asked.

"Good, but the wake up has been a little rough. But I'll be all right. Must have been the wine."

"I thought it was great wine."

"It was. Maybe I shouldn't have ordered that second bottle. How's Mr. Chipper doing?"

"Fine, Mister Larry. Can we play some shuffleboard again today?"

"Don't see why not. My schedule's as open as that ocean out there."

"Good. But don't let me win today, okay? I know you let me win yesterday."

"It's a deal. I'll beat your little butt to turkey mush."

"Larry..."

"Could you pass the cornflakes and pour me a little of that fine Captain's Best coffee?"

"Here."

"We arrive tomorrow, right?"

"Yes, they said at about four-thirty."

"I like it out here."

"I liked it on top of that mountain."

"I liked it on top of ... on top of ..."

"Larry..." She glanced at Chipper.

"How old are you Chipper? I forget."

"Eight."

"Did you like it in Switzerland?"

"You know I did. I already told ya."

"Are you going to stay in touch with Nadia?"

"I already told ya that too."

"She was one gorgeous female. You've got good taste, just like me."

"Eat your cornflakes, Larry."

"Yes dear."

When the trio went up on the recreation deck for shuffleboard the morning sky was tagged with low cotton ball clouds and it seemed the only wind came from the speed of the boat. Tammy dropped into a chaise longue and watched her son and Farley push the plastic disks towards the triangle of numbers. They said "I gotcha!",

"Oh no!", "Take that!", "Good shot!", and "Yes!" and Tammy closed her eyes. She thought of Betty Swain's body in a long refrigerator with frost on her eyebrows, hair, and purple lips. For a minute she could think of nothing else except eighty years of life coming to that. She thought the toes and fingers were probably frozen and if you bumped one it would probably break off. Then, for whatever reason, she thought of the pre-flood world and the millions of people who had seen God, had talked to God, had felt God within them, in their bosom as sure as blood, and who had lived happily and unhappily in a paint-by-numbers world.

That world was gone.

37

In the year 3 A.F. funerals were not held in churches; they were held anywhere. Hence they could be open affairs where strollers or passers-by might stop, watch awhile, and move on. Betty Swain's was in the park where she and Tammy used to sit and talk. Her coffin was small and, at Tammy's request, had been painted by Chipper and the other children who were to dance and sing around it. There were trees and flowers and large-headed, thin-limbed animals and people. There was one house with a door, a window, and a chimney and a smiling sun within a powder blue sky. Billy B, Bill the policeman, Olga, Philip Papp, his son Jay, and Farley had carried the box and Betty from the morgue to the park, a little less than three blocks. Tammy had procured two wooden crates that the coffin was laid on. A few people had followed the pallbearers down the sidewalk and into the park and were waiting for the ceremony, some standing close, others on benches.

Tammy had rounded up twelve children from the neighbourhood and had taught them the two songs. They were dressed in matching shorts and T-shirts, each child wearing a different colour. They stood around the box holding hands and most were smiling. Betty had requested that it be a happy occasion. Betty's close friends and acquaintances made a larger circle outside of the children.

It was Farley who raised his hand and got everyone's attention and quiet. You could hear birds warble, then Tammy said, "For eighty years Betty Swain lived and loved. Before dying she asked for children to sing these two songs." Tammy waved a finger in the warm summer air and the children danced anti-clockwise and sang.

Happy deathday to you!
Happy deathday to you!
Happy deathday dear Betty,
Happy deathday to you!

And then:

Row, row, row your boat,
Gently down the stream
Merrily, merrily, merrily, merrily,
Life is but a dream.

The children's voices rang strong and clear, surely as Betty would have wanted. They only sang it once. With no church, there was no seasoned organist – with eyebrows raised, mouth open, and hands poised – to nod the singers into a reprise.

38

Of course, they all went to Billy B's after they had tucked Betty in bed for good. They chatted about Betty and the World Visionary Council and what had happened at home while Tammy and Farley were away. I was surprised at the mood. I had thought it would be festive, but it wasn't. When no one believes in heaven or hell, death can be extremely heavy, like a bag of cement. Betty, I must say, took it like a champion. But the truth is, she was rather tired of living. Philip Papp, brave soul that he is, cried a lot. He knew that the deceased had been as good to him as a person can be. His son Jay, having separated with his girlfriend, had come up a week earlier from Florida. He'd had to do something with his broken heart, so he brought it north to his dad. Since Violetta left him, I have observed him quite carefully and noted latent bubblings of human desperation. I wonder where they might lead.

Jon Ferguson was born in October 1949 in Oakland, California, into a devout Christian family, much like his favourite philosopher, Friedrich Nietzsche. In fact, as a child, church services were held in the family living room. At age 17, his passion for sport was almost usurped by a keenness to save the world when he enrolled at Brigham Young University. Little by little, though, he realised that if Jesus couldn't do it, neither could he. His faith in divinity began to crumble. With an adieu to the US academic world where he'd been immersed in anthropology and philosophy – and with a desire to engage with the world at large – Ferguson hopped on a plane in 1973 and by chance ended up in Nyon, Switzerland where he was soon playing basketball in the top Swiss league, becoming a key player in what fans consider to have been the golden age.

Half a century later he is now just as well known for his writing (eighteen books published in French) as for his coaching (thirty years' worth). He won more games than any coach in Swiss basketball history, but he likes to remind people that he lost more than everyone else as well... He has written over twenty novels and a book on Nietzsche, *Nietzsche au Petit Déjeuner* ("Nietzsche for Breakfast") and a book on the history of Swiss basketball, *Of Hoops and Men*. For twenty-five years he also wrote a bi-weekly column in the Lausanne newspaper called "Ainsi Parla Schmaltz". His novel *Farley's Jewel* (Cinco Puntos Press, 1998) won a Barnes & Noble "Discover Great New Writers of America" prize.

More by Jon Ferguson

Foster's Depression
Adam's Cane
Jesus & Mary
Mary & God
God & Naomi
The Flood

Available soon:

The Old Man and the Sea
Don't Bullshit Me Daddy
The Anthropologist
Farley's Jewel

Sign up to receive updates on this author's titles at
www.jonfergusonbooks.com and download the
short story *The Last Day Forever* for free.

Lightning Source UK Ltd.
Milton Keynes UK
UKHW012027270522
403631UK00001B/3

9 781911 249900